BASIN PAR
INTERVIEWS WITH THE GHOSTS
by
Juergen E. Schroeder

Juergen Elshroeder

This is a work of fiction, but all of the stories were inspired by the guests of the 1905 Basin Park Hotel who reported their unexplainable experiences. The ghostly apparitions are as they were described by the guests of the hotel. Their names and their stories have no basis in fact or history with the exception of the history of the cowboy, John Chisum.

Front and back cover photos are courtesy of the Basin Park Hotel.

This book is dedicated to the many wonderful guests of the Basin park Hotel. It has been a pleasure serving you over the years, and hearing your wonderful stories.

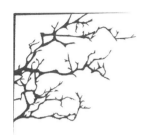

CHAPTER 1

It was the end of August in the year 2019 when Harold entered the 1905 Basin Park Hotel. He glanced around the lobby as he stepped inside, taking note of the fireplace on his right and a display hutch on his left that was filled with souvenirs and T-shirts. The front desk was right in front of him. He noted the old-fashioned pigeon-hole style key boxes that were on the wall behind the front desk. The two-story high ceiling didn't go unnoticed, and neither did the support column that was in the middle of the lobby.

He stepped up to the front desk where a middle-aged lady was on the phone, taking a reservation. The name tag on the lady's shirt identified her as Lynnette. She wore a black, button-up shirt with the Basin Park Hotel logo on the breast pocket, with black pants and hair that was starting to fade to gray. Harold waited patiently until she hung up the phone and finished entering a few keystrokes into her computer, then looked up at him with a smile.

"Hello, Lynnette," he said. "And how might you be this morning?"

"Why, I'm fine, sir, and yourself?"

"I'm doing quite well, thank you. My name is Harold Sangarius, and I'm delighted to pay a visit to your wonderful hotel."

"Well, thank you, Mr. Sangarius. What can I do for you, sir?"

"Well, I would like to speak to your manager about renting the hotel for an extended period of time."

Lynnette's eyebrows rose slightly. "Well, that would be Mr. Rich, he's the manager. Let me give him a call for you. He's upstairs, you can take a seat on the couch while you wait for him to come down."

Harold turned and looked at the sofa, an antique Scofield which was made around the middle of the last century. It had a solid wooden frame with green cushions, and many people had offered to buy this unique piece of furniture.

It didn't take long for Mr. Rich to come downstairs into the lobby. He was dressed in what Harold would come to think of as his usual style, wearing a light purple shirt with a matching tie, black trousers and black shoes. He went directly to the front desk and Lynnette pointed to Harold.

Mr. Rich looked him over. Harold was dressed in a dark gray business suit, with a white shirt, blue tie and black shoes. His dark hair was cropped short and neat about the ears and above the collar. Mr. Rich approached him with a smile, holding out a hand.

"Mr. Sangarius, how do you do? My name is Curry Rich. I'm the room's division manager. What can I do for you?"

"Mr. Rich, I'm Harold Sangarius. I'm an intuitive, professional paranormal investigator, and I would like to rent your entire hotel for four weeks."

Curry was a little surprised at such a request, and his eyes went wide. "Forgive me, did you just say you want to rent the whole hotel for an entire month?"

"I did, yes," Harold said. "You seem a little surprised at my request."

"It certainly is one I've never heard before," Rich said. "I think we should ask Mr. Matthews, our general manager, to join us for this conversation."

"That'll be fine," Harold replied. "Is he available today?"

"Oh, yes," Rich said. "Give me just a moment to call him and ask him to join us." He quickly reached for his cell phone, called Jason Matthews and explained the situation to him.

Rich turned to Harold a moment later and said, "Mr. Matthews will be free to join us in just a few minutes. I hope you don't mind waiting, this is certainly something he would have to handle."

"Not at all," he answered.

Jason Matthews entered the lobby of the Basin Park Hotel wearing a gray T-shirt with the emblem of the 1886 Crescent Hotel, which was owned by the same company. He sported a full head of hair that was starting to turn gray, and he had an air of authority about him. He was the manager of both the 1886 Crescent Hotel and the 1905 Basin Park Hotel. He stepped over to the couch where Curry and Harold were waiting for him.

"Mr. Sangarius, I'm Jason Matthews, the general manager. Let's go up to the first floor, to the Atrium room, where we can talk with some privacy."

Jason, followed by Harold and with Curry bringing up the rear, climbed up the stairs to the first floor and then turned left, leading the way to the Atrium Room. Here, there were a couple of tables covered with white table cloths and set up with chairs around them. The three men sat around the table.

Harold looked around the Atrium room as he followed Mr. Matthews. All around the walls were glass cases displaying Eureka Springs and Basin Park Hotel memorabilia. The glass roof showed a clear blue sky overhead.

Jason Matthews turned to Harold and curiously said, "Sangarius. That is an usual last name."

"Yes, I have been told that many times," chuckled Harold. "My parents told me that we are descendants of a Greek god called Sangarius, who was the lesser god of the rivers. As far as I know, my mother has always talked to spirits and my grandmother as well. I fear that I inherited the ability, and so I'm following in their footsteps."

Jason asked, "Very interesting. So, Mr. Sangarius, you say you are interested in renting the entire hotel for four weeks?"

"That's right," Harold said. "I'm a professional intuitive paranormal investigator from The Institute of Paranormal Studies, which is headquartered in Salem, Massachusetts. I want to do a thorough investigation on the paranormal activities in the Basin Park Hotel. I must say that I have stayed at both the Crescent Hotel, which is identified as the most haunted hotel in America, and at the Basin Park Hotel, which doesn't seem to get much recognition as a haunted hotel, but I found a more interesting paranormal experience at the Basin Park than I did at the Crescent. I would like to rent the entire Hotel for four weeks so that my investigation can be undisturbed by other people who might create an adverse condition that could interfere with my communicating with the spirits here in the Basin Park Hotel."

"And when did you want to rent the hotel?" asked Curry.

Harold smiled. "At your earliest possible convenience."

"January is the slowest month of the year," Jason said. "The first weekend in January, we close the hotel on Sunday to all guests because that is our usual paranormal weekend. On that day we have all kinds of paranormal investigators touring the hotel, trying to find evidence that both the Crescent and the Basin are haunted."

"Oh, I'm afraid that would not do," Harold replied. "I would absolutely have to have the place all to myself, which is why I'm willing to rent the entire hotel."

Rich frowned. "We generally sell out, or are very close to it on the weekends even in January, Mr. Sangarius. We already have reservations for the weekends well into February, and we are always sold out for Valentine's Day weekend."

"Mr. Rich," Harold said, "I don't think you understand. Money is no object. The Institute for Paranormal Studies will pay whatever it takes, even the higher weekend rates."

"Well," Rich said, "that could present a problem. You see, many of our guests on the weekends are regulars, and it seems that it would be inconsiderate for us to cancel their reservations. We could attempt to contact them to see if they would be willing to move to the Crescent, but we couldn't guarantee that they'll go along with it."

Jason pursed his lips and laid a hand on Rich's arm. "We could close the hotel on Sunday after everyone has checked out, but we would have to reopen Friday morning. In January we don't get a lot of weekday traffic and it will be much easier to move anyone who has reservations for the weekday to the Crescent Hotel. On Sunday we would have housekeepers here until at least 1 PM, because they would have to strip the dirty linens from all the rooms. Then there is our restaurant, which is open in the winter from noon to 6 PM. We also have to man the front desk 24 hours a day, and we have a bellman on duty from 8 AM to 10 PM during the winter months. We would probably also have to have a housekeeper on hand during the day to wash the dirty laundry. That would be the least disruptive to our regular guests, if that might be acceptable to you."

"I can understand that you don't want to alienate your regular guests. And I can understand why you need someone to man the front desk. I will accept your terms for renting the hotel from Sunday afternoon at 1 o'clock through Friday morning but I must insist that all employees that are working must not leave the lobby level during that time. We will even pay to have the restaurant stay closed, and we will also compensate the employees who would normally be working - it will be like they're being paid to stay home."

"That means that you will start renting the hotel on January 9, the day after the paranormal weekend," said Jason.

"And you can rent the hotel through February 10 when Valentine's weekend begins," added Rich. "Also, since it is January, it is possible that we may have bad weather that would prevent our employees from going home and returning to work. We normally allow our employees on these occasions to spend the night. If that should happen, we can put them in our specialty suites on the mezzanine floor so as to create the least amount of interruptions to your investigation. And our time clock is on the first floor, so those that are working will have to go to the first floor to clock in."

"No," Harold said, "I'm afraid that simply won't do. Can't they log their time at the front desk, instead?"

"Yes, of course they can," responded Jason. "That will solve that problem."

"In that case, gentlemen, I can accept your terms," Harold said. "I will see you all on January 9, and I will be staying for four weeks. That means that I will be checking out on February 5. I will also need the same room for the entire 28 days that I will be here."

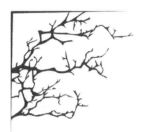

CHAPTER 2

On January 9, right on schedule, Harold Sangarius entered the lobby of the Basin Park Hotel bright and early at 8 AM. "Good morning, Lynnette," he said to the smiling lady behind the desk.

"Good morning, Mr. Sangarius," she replied, matching his smile. "We've all been waiting excitedly for your visit."

"You are so kind," he said. "I was thinking, since I will be needing access to all the rooms in the hotel, would you have a master key that works for all of them? Or, perhaps you can have someone unlock all the rooms?"

"I can have the bellman unlock all the doors for you," Lynette replied. "There are actually several different master keys, and they can be confusing."

"That would be wonderful. Do you have a particular room assigned to me, for my own use?"

"We can give you one of the specially suites on the mezzanine floor, or we can give you a Queen Jacuzzi suite. Those are located on the third, fourth and fifth floors, so you can take your pick." She grinned. "Since you're renting the entire hotel, it's up to you which room you want to stay in."

"Since the third floor seems to be the most active floor, I'll take one of the suites there." His eyes twinkled. "Might as well be in the thick of it, eh?"

"Okay, then, let's put you in Room 317. Do you need the bellman to help you with your luggage?"

"Oh, No," Harold said, "I can take care of it myself. And please remember, after the bellman unlocks all the doors, no one should leave the lobby level."

"Yes, Mr. Matthews made sure we all understood your instructions," Lynnette replied. "You will need to move your vehicle down to our parking lot after you get your luggage inside. Do you know where it is?"

"Yes," Harold said. "Let me bring my things in now, and then I will be right down to get my vehicle moved."

"Okay. Since you are the only guests, I'll have the bellman follow you down with our shuttle, to drive you back up here."

"Wonderful."

It didn't take Harold long to get his car parked and get settled into his room. As soon as he had done so, he grabbed up his video camera and a digital recorder and began to roam the hotel. He could sense entities all around him, and a few times he was sure that he saw some orbs flying in the halls (an ability that he was sure he had inherited from his mother, who used to report seeing them quite often).

He decided to work from the top down, so he took the elevator all the way to the top floor. He felt a sense of excitement as he stepped out of the elevator, and realize quickly that he was in for an adventure.

As he entered the Atrium room, on the first floor, he saw a woman seated at one of the tables. She wore a white gown reminiscent of the late 1800's. If she were flesh and bone, one would have described her face as angelic, and her figure as one that a model would die for, but her body was translucent and her eyes black like coal. Her dark red hair was long and slightly wavy as it draped over her shoulder, and would be considered shiny and glowing if you couldn't see right through it. Her lips seemed as red as a ruby, and her voice, when she spoke, sounded like sweet honey.

Harold remembered that quite a few guests had reported seeing a ghostly image of a woman with red hair. In all of those encounters, however, she had never seemed to appear but for a few seconds.

"I have been waiting for you, Harold," Harold heard the woman say. "And what is that thing you have in your hands?"

"This is a digital audio recorder. It will allow me to record our conversation so that I will have a record of what we talk about today."

She smiled. "Are you sure that it will record the voice of the dead?"

"It has before, but this is the first time I have heard one of your voices so clearly. Perhaps we should test to be sure? Let me turn it on and then if you would say a few words..."

"Mary had a little lamb," recited the redhead, a mischievous smile on her face.

Harold stopped the recorder, rewound it and hit the play button. As the recorder played, the redheaded woman heard her own voice saying, "Mary had a little lamb."

"See," Harold said. "It did record your voice."

"Yes," she said, "but did you know that we have the power to erase your recording? We can even drain its batteries."

Harold gave her a wry grin. "Yes, I have seen such things happen in some of my other paranormal investigations," he said, "but if you are willing to tell me your story, then destroying the recording would defeat the purpose. I would be able to recall some things from memory but probably not everything, and I would like to be able to refer back to the recording for the sake of accuracy." Harold said. He set the recorder on the table and turned it on so they could begin the interview.

Suddenly, as Harold was about to begin speaking with this beautiful, ghostly woman, he watched her translucent form turn opaque. He had never encountered such a transformation. This ghostly entity now appeared as solid as a living, flesh and blood woman.

"How is it you know my name?" he asked.

"We all know your name," smiled the entity.

"All of you know who I am?" Harold asked, his eyebrows rising in surprise.

"Yes," she said. "Many of us were present at your meeting with Mr. Matthews. We have all been anxiously awaiting your arrival."

"Many? How many spirits live here in the hotel?"

"I don't think I really know the answer to that question. We never took a head count. I do know that our cowboy, John, is most anxious to talk to you."

"John, the cowboy?" Harold asked; his own excitement obvious in his voice. "Would that be John Chisum? The one who was a part of the Lincoln County wars, and was involved with Billy the Kid? I know that some people think the cowboy is John Chisum, but is it really him?"

"Yes, the one and the same. He will meet you when he is ready, at the appointed time. I know John quite well; we have spent over 100 years together here at the Basin Park Hotel. He is a tall, kindly gentleman that truly cares about other people and about always doing the right thing. He is kind and gentle and highly courageous. He is very honorable and a true gentleman in the southern fashion."

"And who, may I ask, am I speaking to?" Harold asked.

"My name is Charlotte."

"Do you have a last name?"

"My full name is Charlotte Ann Prichard."

"And where are you from, Charlotte?" Harold asked. "I believe I detect a southern accent."

She smiled again. "You do, indeed. I was born and raised in Savannah, Georgia."

"And how is it that you were expecting me?"

"Oh," Charlotte said, her smile growing, "we in the spirit world have heard many good things about you. Word of your coming to the Basin Park Hotel has been rumored on the spiritual airwaves for quite some time, and then you made the rumors come true when you booked your reservation back in August."

"Spiritual airwaves!" Harold said, grinning. "I like that. The allies could have used you in World War 1 and World War 2."

"Yes, but not very many people are receptive to the spiritual world. Most people walk around in oblivion, focusing strictly on what is in front of them and with their daily lives. Most are not aware of what is going on in their own physical world, and therefore have no clue, nor do they care, what goes on in the spiritual. However, just like in your physical world, we in the spirit world also have our degrees of good and evil."

"Yes," Harold said, "quite true. And what brought you to Eureka Springs, Arkansas, and the Basin Park Hotel?"

"It wasn't the Basin Park Hotel when I came to Eureka Springs," Charlotte said. "My husband, Alexander Travis Prichard, and I were staying in the Perry House, which was the luxury hotel in Eureka Springs at that time. The Basin Park Hotel was built on the same footprint as the Perry House. The Perry House burnt down in 1890. I was very sick at the time, and my husband brought me to Eureka Springs for the healing springs we had heard so much about."

"It would seem that the healing springs were not very healing," Harold said.

Charlotte gave a polite shrug. "When we got settled in our room at the Perry House, my husband sent for the doctor. The doctor recommended that I drink at least three glasses of water from the springs each day, and that I take a soaking bath in spring water at least once a day. And, to be honest, my health started to improve. Day by day I started to feel a little better but after two weeks my health started failing me again."

"So the healing springs were improving your health, but maybe it was too much of a good thing? So, is it safe to conclude that the water from the healing springs were the cause of your death?"

"Oh, no, certainly not," Charlotte said. "The healing springs were doing what they claimed to do, but there were other factors that caused my death. I didn't know it at the time but my death was not accidental. They say that no one died in the Perry House but that is not true. I died here and have been here ever since."

"Your death was not an accident, or just from illness?" Harold asked. "What happened, then?"

"It turns out that my husband had a mistress whom he wanted to marry. He didn't want to divorce me because he would have lost half his wealth. What I found out after I died was that he had been feeding me arsenic in small doses while we were at home in Savannah. It turns out that he had brought his mistress to Eureka Springs at the same time that he brought me. With my health improving, it was creating a complication in his relationship with his mistress. Once my health started to improve, my husband started giving me small doses of arsenic again, which he mixed in the spring waters he brought me, until the end. Even the doctor's death certificate listed me as having died of natural causes." She paused for a moment and then smiled at him saying, "They told my poor husband that he simply brought me here too late."

"So, no one ever knew that you had been murdered?"

"No," answered Charlotte. "No one ever knew, other than my friends here. You are the first living person to whom I have ever been able to tell that story."

"And what became of your husband and his mistress?" Harold asked.

"They were married right here in Eureka Springs two weeks after I was buried. I would have loved to have haunted them for the rest of their lives but they moved back to Savannah and I was stuck here in the Perry House, until it burned down and later became the Basin Park Hotel. They never returned to Eureka Springs." A sadness came into her eyes. "I never would have believed that my husband would murder me. I loved him so very much and I thought he felt the same way about me. If he was going to murder me, I wish he had found a less cruel way to do it. I suffered for a long time while the arsenic was destroying my body. The pain was so unbearable that the doctor started giving me morphine, which in the end did little to lessen the agony."

"This is so tragic," Harold said. "I'm so sorry this happened to you."

Once again, she shrugged. "At the time I was too sick to know what was going on. I don't know how the doctor missed all the symptoms. I don't understand why Dr. Paul Bull didn't pick up on all my symptoms; they were classic arsenic symptoms: headaches, diarrhea, vomiting, vomiting blood, blood in the urine, cramping muscles, hair loss, stomach pain and convulsions. My lungs, skin, kidneys and liver were all affected by the arsenic poisoning, and it was even visible within the pigmentation of my fingernails. He just kept on saying that I needed to drink more of the water and take more baths." She sighed. "I confessed to wandering if he was persuaded to not notice those signs. Dr. Bull was middle-aged and skinny as a rail, and God knows doctors didn't earn very much back then. A greasing of the palms may have persuaded him to look the other way."

"It makes me wonder why your husband ever married you in the first place," Harold said. "You appear quite young; surely you couldn't have been married very long."

"I was only twenty and six when I died. As for the reason for my marriage, I've had many years to consider that question. Harold, my father and mother were quite well off financially. Back then, some even called us wealthy. I've come to the conclusion that Alexander did the fashionable thing and married me for my money. I was an only child, so I would have inherited quite a bit of money when my parents died. I'm almost positive that with my death, my parents would have left their fortune to Alexander, especially since they didn't know that he had murdered me."

"A tragic story indeed, but quite fascinating," Harold licked his lips and then looked at her again. "So, what was Eureka Springs like back then?"

"Eureka Springs was a very unique place, even in those days. There were a lot of bathhouses, and thousands of people flocked here for the healing spring water. There were two big hotels downtown at the time, the Southern and the Perry House, and both were always packed to overflowing. The Perry House was by far the most luxurious hotel in town. The town was packed with people from the rich and well-to-do to paupers dressed in rags, all coming here to be healed by the spring waters, and, I'm sure, some with ill intentions on their mind. Business was booming and there were many new buildings under construction. There were beautiful homes being built, as well as many shanties, so the trees were being cut down in record numbers on the hills. The mountains turned from being a beautiful forest to a denuded hillside. And when the rains came, the mud from the hillsides flowed like a thick river of brown sludge down into Main Street, which, at that time, was simply called Mud Street. There was so much mud that, overtime, it raised Mud Street up one floor level and the second floor of the buildings became the first floor. Today, Mud Street is named Main Street."

"I've heard of things like that," Harold said. "The original first floor becomes like a basement."

"Yes. Back in the 1880s there was also a small Indian village where the Indians insisted on living in their teepees made of hides. They insisted on living in their old ways and would not consider building wooden homes, but they were quite civilized. Of course, I'm speaking of the way the white man would consider civilized, and they were very helpful in teaching people the ways of the healing waters."

"I'm sure they would have known about them for a long time," Harold said.

"Oh, they did indeed. Of course! They were very much a part of Eureka Springs." Charlotte took a deep breath before continuing. "In the town, there were many handsome carriages lining the streets as well as many freight wagons transporting lumber and trade goods all along Mud Street and Spring Street. And there was countless horse traffic everywhere. Then in the late 1880s, Eureka Springs was devastated by many fires. You see, many places had upgraded to the new gas lighting system, but very few took the time to install the gas lighting system in a safe manner. Many of them only had small gas pipes with an open flame."

"An obvious prescription for disaster," Harold agreed.

"We arrived in Eureka Springs in the summer of 1887. The Perry House was a four-story structure and its luxury was such to rival any of the best hotels in the East, from New York City to Savannah. Back in those days, there was only one water closet on each floor, just as it was in the finest hotels in the East. I loved the Perry House, but frankly, I prefer the Basin Park Hotel. It's not that its luxury rivals the Perry House, but for the fact that it has a bathroom in each room giving people the privacy that they didn't have back then. In 1890, the

Perry House became a victim of the fires, itself. They say that no one died in that fire, but the fire was so intense that no one really knows if that is true or not. I consider myself fortunate that I had died before that fire began; otherwise I would surely have been caught in that inferno."

Harold thought for a moment before he asked, "Why is it that you never left the Basin Park Hotel rather than returning, say, to your hometown of Savannah?"

"Oh, how I loved Savannah. I was born and raised there and Alex, my husband, was also born and raised in Savannah. We had a beautiful plantation where we grew mostly cotton and tobacco. We were very prosperous and happy there. We were always invited to the most prestigious parties." Charlotte's face appeared sad as she reminisced. "I loved seeing all the old mansions with their multitude of columns rising from the porches. And I do miss all my old friends who were near and dear to me, friends that I had grown up with. I often think of Savannah and the life I had there, with its cobblestone streets and the breeze coming in from the ocean, and the smell of the salty sea. I had servants back there that took care of my every need and desire; I loved them and I like to think that they loved me in return; they were so kind and considerate. I was so glad that slavery had ended because then I knew that my servants truly cared about me and were not serving under the threat of duress. I considered returning to my beautiful Savannah, but the thought of seeing my husband with his new wife was more than I could bear. So here is where I decided to stay."

"Savannah didn't fair too well during Sherman's march to the sea, did it?" Harold asked.

"No. Sherman destroyed my family's plantation. And then the northern carpetbaggers tried to steal our land with their outrageous taxes. We would have lost everything if it had not been for my father's foresight. My father didn't trust the bankers. Oh, he used them, but only for what was necessary. My father put his faith in real money, gold and silver, which, he made sure I knew, was the only true currency allowed in the Constitution of 1789. He said Congress was only given the authority to coin money, not to print it. Hence, my father stored a lot of gold and silver coins in the floor under the plantation house in several different locations. We had plenty of money to pay off the greedy thieves and to re-build our home. We were the lucky ones. Most lost everything and their homes were taken over by those unscrupulous northern whores." Anger clearly showed in Charlotte's eyes. "I was only a child, but I remember it well."

"Well," Harold said, "let's get back to our talk about Eureka Springs."

"Yes, that's much easier," Charlotte said. "It was interesting to be here and watch the men building the Basin Park Hotel with all those huge limestone blocks that were delivered using horse-drawn wagons. There was a steady stream of wagons all day long. The builders and their mules struggled to set each stone in place. Back then they didn't have the modern machines that we see today. It took them more than a year to finish building the Basin Park Hotel, but when they finally finished, it had the distinction of being the first building in Eureka Springs with electricity being used for lighting, which was much safer than the gas lighting of the Perry House."

She suddenly looked to her left, and then turned back to Harold.

"And now, Harold, we must suspend our interview. There are others that want to talk to you."

"I find it fascinating to talk to you, Charlotte. Will we be meeting again?" Harold asked.

"That is quite likely." Charlotte smiled and a radiant glow shone all around her.

"I don't see anyone else around who might want to be interviewed," Harold said.

"Oh, they are all around, but you must seek them out. We will not be lined up in a row waiting for our turn at an interview, but, if you seek, then you shall find." With those words, she disappeared before Harold's eyes, and Harold watched as her light very slowly faded.

Turning off the recorder, Harold continued to sit in the Atrium room for several long minutes thinking about the long talk he had with Charlotte, but that was not all he was thinking about. He marveled at Charlotte's beauty and how attractive she was. He also thought of what a terrible shame that such a lovely and charming woman's life had been cut short in the name of money. Finally, he stood up and continued wondering through the hotel.

Slowly, Harold meandered through every room on every floor of the hotel. Many times he saw orbs flying through the rooms and in the halls, but no other spirit showed itself to him. After hours of searching, Harold finally returned to his room and began the work of transcribing the recording of Charlotte's interview.

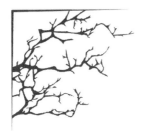

CHAPTER 3

The next day, Monday, Harold roamed every floor, and every room on every floor of the hotel. He would take the elevator up to the sixth floor and work his way down from there. He did this constantly throughout the day. He even carried an EMF meter with him, and whenever there was a spike on the meter, he would call out with the hope that someone would appear and talk to him. Late that evening he gave up on his search and returned to his room, where he quickly heated a meal in the microwave before retiring to his bed, exhausted.

Tuesday was a repeat of Monday. Harold could not understand why he had such a terrific interview with Charlotte that very first day and then nothing, even though there was an indication from Charlotte that others were willing to talk to him. Even so, Harold slowly and diligently scoured the hotel looking for someone else to interview but found no one.

Wednesday morning dawned with a snow-covered mantle all over the ground. It brought a chill into the room and Harold cranked up the temperature on his room's heating/air conditioning units. After preparing himself a meager breakfast, Harold scoured through the hotel once again. After his exciting interview on Sunday, Harold was getting a little discouraged when he ended his tour in the lobby. He saw Lynnette sitting behind the front desk and decided to talk to her, hoping to glean more information about the ghosts in the hotel, and maybe she had stories that he had not heard before.

Even this was disappointing and after an hour, Harold, discouraged, once again stepped into the elevator and pushed the button for the sixth floor for his second round through the hotel. As he stepped out of the elevator, he looked around the foyer. In front of him were the stained-glass windows that overlooked Eureka Springs. Walking up to the windows, he had a good view of the town covered in a pure white blanket. He moved off to the right and entered the Lucky Seven Bar and Billiard room. He opened the door into a wide passageway with storage closets on the right and the left. Walking past these, he entered the bar and billiard area. There were two billiard tables to his right on a raised platform, and on the left were a couch and several tables and chairs. Stained-glass windows lined the left side of the room and overlooked the Basin Spring Park. On the windowsills were stacks of board games. In the far left corner was the bar.

Further down on the right, after the billiard tables, there was a foosball machine. He also saw two dartboards hanging on doors to other closeted areas. In the back, he saw a double door leading out onto the fire escape. He knew from reading *Ripley's Believe It Or Not* that the Basin Park Hotel was the only hotel in the world where every floor was a ground-floor. He had seen for himself that this was true because every fire exit from every floor on the south side of the hotel led out into the cliff behind the building.

Finding nothing, Harold left the Lucky Seven Bar and Billiard room. He walked through the foyer to the Barefoot Ballroom on the north side of the hotel. (The Barefoot Ballroom's name was inspired by the appearance of Mr. and Mrs. Howard Forehan of Santa Ana, California, who came to Eureka Springs on a honeymoon financed by the "Truth or Consequences" radio show on the condition that they wear no shoes during the trip. At the end of a week's visit, Manager Joe Parkhill of the Basin Park Hotel originated the Barefoot Ballroom in their honor.) There was a double door entrance to the ballroom. Inside the ballroom, on the right, was an elevated stage. The rest of the room was a huge open area with stained-glass windows all around. At the back of the room was a double door fire escape. Per Harold's request, several tables and chairs had been set up in the room.

Harold made his way to the ballroom and as he opened up the door he saw a man and woman sitting in chairs around one of the tables.

They were both dressed in elegant evening attire. The man wore a black tuxedo and a black top hat with a white shirt and a black string tie. The woman wore a gold evening gown that covered her from her neck to her ankles; short puffy sleeves reached almost down to her elbows; her dark brown hair was cut shoulder length and beautifully framed her face.

"Hello," Harold said. Excitement was clearly evident in his voice.

"Hello, Harold," replied the gentleman.

"I was beginning to wonder if I would see any of you again," Harold said. "I have been searching ever since my interview with Charlotte on Sunday."

"Patience is a virtue, Harold," said the woman, with a sly smile. "As a man of science, you should know that."

"Yes, but patience is a virtue that is hard to attain for mankind. We have been indoctrinated with the idea of instant gratification in this day and age. And what, may I ask, are your names?"

"Have a seat, Harold, and if you like, you may turn your recorder on." The couple waited until Harold set his recorder on the table and pushed the record button. "My name is Simon Garfield, and this is my wife, Mildred," answered the gentleman.

"One of the nighttime front desk clerks," Harold said, "said that on several occasions he saw a ghostly apparition of a man and a woman walking down the stairs to the lobby. They always walked to the window overlooking Spring Street. The front desk clerk reported that they stood at the window for a while before disappearing. Are you the couple he saw?"

"Yes, we are. We only allow ourselves to be seen occasionally, but we have also been seen by others besides the evening front desk clerk. Mildred, do you remember the time when we were dancing in the Ozark room while a large group from the ghost tour entered the room?" asked Simon.

"Oh, my, yes I do," Mildred said with a smile. "There were two people in the group that had what they called iPads. One had a new one and one had an old one. It was kind of funny; the new one couldn't pick up a thing, but the old one caught all of us in the room dancing. The whole ghost tour group stood and watched the screen of the device for almost thirty minutes while the room was filled with dancers. I often wondered if the man with the old iPad had recorded a video of us."

"Fascinating," Harold said. "Was it a special occasion that brought you all to the dance?"

"No, not at all," Simon replied. "We all love to dance and we do so often. Sometimes, when Mildred and I want to take a short break from the dancing, we would walk down to the lobby and stand looking out into the street where we reminisce about days gone by."

"So, what is it that brought you and Mildred to Eureka Springs?" Harold asked.

Mildred smiled. "We had heard so much about the town. We had heard about the healing waters. Our son, George, was sick and the doctors were not able to help him. So we brought our son to Eureka Springs and we praise God for the healing springs because they did heal George. The healing took about ninety days and once George was healed, we decided to take some extra time to see the town. You see, while George was sick, we never got a chance to look around because all our time was spent looking after George."

"Yes, it was quite a stressful time," Simon said. "We were so worried about George. When his health started to improve, we started to relax a little bit. When George was fully recovered, we decided it was time for a real vacation."

Harold paid close attention to his guests. He asked, "So the healing springs were doing what people claimed they could do?"

"Oh, yes," Mildred said, smiling again. "So much so, that we wrote many a letter to friends and family proclaiming the miracles of the Eureka Springs waters."

"But there is obviously much more to your story," Harold said. "For example, where are you from; how did you come to haunt the Basin Park Hotel; and what happened to your son, George?"

Simon began telling the story. "We were both born and raised in Boston. It was an exciting time as the new century was approaching. I was the owner of the Boston Independent Bank."

Mildred added, "And Simon was very successful running his bank. I was born to a banking family and Simon was a success even before we were married. I wasn't really interested in Simon when we met, but both my parents kept pressuring me into pursuing Simon. We could all tell that Simon was attracted to me, but frankly, I didn't feel very interested in him. I actually married Simon because of the pressure put on me by my mother and father. And the truth be told, I never regretted it. Simon was and is the love of my life." She looked at him, and her eyes reflected the emotion she was describing.

"Just as Mildred is the love of my life," added Simon. "The bank no longer exists, but Mildred and I have an eternity to share our love with each other."

"Amen," replied Mildred with enthusiasm. "We were so enjoying the sights of Eureka Springs and taking buggy rides throughout the town that it was a shame that tragedy struck us without warning. George was in the park playing with other children. We thank God that he was not with us at the time of our impending doom. We were walking down Spring Street, on our way to Mud Street to visit the shops there. The freighters were hauling huge limestone blocks for the construction of the Basin Park Hotel. It took eight mules to haul the heavily loaded wagons. It all happened so suddenly that we were not aware of the tragedy that was about to befall us. We didn't have time to get out of the way. As the freighter set the brakes on his wagon, the brake lock failed and the wagon began to roll backwards down the street. We didn't pay any attention to the noise because there was nothing unusual about it until we heard the workman shouting out in warning. We both turned to look to see what they were shouting about, but it was too late. As we turned to see what the warning was about, the wagon crashed into us and that was the end of our mortal existence."

Harold thought that he might have seen some tears running down Mildred's cheeks as she remembered that terrible tragedy.

"It took us a few minutes to die," said Simon, "but we died holding each other's hands."

"I take it that George witnessed the tragedy?" Harold asked.

"George may have not actually seen what happened, but he certainly saw the results, his mother and father lying crushed beneath a wagon full of limestone blocks. The workman had rushed to the scene and they had to hold George back from coming to take a closer look at our deformed state." Harold could hear the pain and sadness in Simon's voice.

"What happened to George?"

Mildred answered saying, "We were staying at the Southern Hotel, which was the finest hotel downtown, after the Perry House burned down. The staff there was very good and they all knew George. After we died, the staff looked after George until his uncle, Samuel Garfield, came to pick him up and take him back to Boston." Proudly Mildred added, "There he became a very successful stockbroker."

"Why is it that you stayed downtown at the Southern Hotel instead of the newer, more prestigious 1886 Crescent Hotel?" Harold asked.

Simon answered. "We certainly considered it, but decided to stay close to the healing waters and to the doctors. The closest spring to the Crescent Hotel is the Grotto spring which is in a cave and just drips water along the walls; not ideal for soaking in the spring water."

"So how long have you been in the Basin Park Hotel?"

"We came to the Basin even before it opened up the doors in 1905. We stayed at the Southern Hotel until Samuel left with George to head back east. Then we decided that it was only fitting and proper that since our death was caused by the Basin Park Hotel that we would stay there. We actually never haunted anyone. We mostly stay to ourselves and simply bask in the love we share. We always attend the dances and talk with many of the long term spiritual residents in the hotel."

"The dances?" Harold asked. "Who plans the dances and do you have one every night?"

"My goodness," laughed Mildred. "Not every night. That would be too exhausting. I do so love helping to plan them. Sometimes we might have one a week and sometimes every two weeks. Then again, there are times it is less often."

"Many of us love to dance," added Simon.

"Do you know why the other spirits came to live in the Basin?"

"Each one of us has our own reasons for choosing to live here. Some of them chose the Basin because of the friendliness of the other spirits who live here. There are no poltergeists here, because we chase them away. We don't want them living with us."

"Have any of you ever talked with other paranormal investigators, like the people that come searching the hotel during their ESP, paranormal weekend?" Harold asked.

"Some of us have been tempted to talk to them, but many of them are more interested in the spirits at the Crescent Hotel and only seem to make a show of investigating the Basin. We took a vote and decided not to talk to them, but to just give them the feel of our presence," answered Simon. "We know that some of the investigators are truly interested in talking to us, but like any good democracy, the majority rules."

"Yet here you are talking to me. Was that a democratic decision?"

"Absolutely," smiled Simon.

"Why me? Why not one of the other paranormal investigators?" Harold asked.

"You have quite a reputation in the spiritual world, Harold. We are all aware of your work and the sincere investigations done at the Institute of Paranormal Studies. You are the only one most of us have agreed to talk to," Simon said.

"So, some of you voted 'NO'?"

"In any democracy, it is extremely rare to get everyone to agree. Still, the majority rules."

"I guess that means that I won't be talking to all the spirits in the Basin?"

"No. You won't, but you also won't be talking to many that voted in favor of us speaking to you."

"Oh," paused Harold.

"So are either of you the ones who moved the toiletry articles around in the rooms or levitated books?" Harold asked.

"Oh," laughed Mildred. "Oh, that's the trickster. I think she should tell you her story herself. We will talk to her and ask her if she is willing to talk to you. She would have many stories to tell you."

"Okay," Harold said. "I heard a story about a night time bellman that was doing his room checks one evening and when he was doing his check of Room 408, he had just left the bedroom and had stepped into the sitting room when the door to the bedroom slammed shut. It took him quite a while to get the door open. He found the bedroom to be ice cold. It gave him a pretty good scare. Is there anything that you can tell me about that?"

"Oh, that was Wilbur," smiled Mildred. "He wants to talk to you during your stay."

"He's not going to freeze me, is he?" joked Harold.

"No, but you may feel a chill in the air," laughed Simon.

"Okay. Can you tell me anything about the stories of the lion and the priest from Room 519? Some say the lion sometimes appears in the door entering the room?"

Mildred laughed as Simon answered. "Again, that is something that the priest will have to tell you."

"Alright then, what about the little girl ghost that I have heard so much about?" Harold asked.

"It is not for us to tell you other people's stories. If they want you to know, then they will tell you," Simon said.

"There was a report from two different people who stayed in Room 417. These reports were months apart. In both cases it was a woman who stayed in the room. Each one heard someone talking right outside their door. When they looked, there was no one there, and they had even looked down the halls to see who it might have been. Do you know anything about that incident?"

Simon frowned, and said, "Yes, we know about that, but the one who did that has declined to talk to you. He is kind of shy, which is why people may hear him but they will never see him."

"Maybe you can confirm another report that I heard?" Harold asked.

"Sure," Simon said. "That is one of the reasons we chose to talk to you."

"The story is that in 2012, a husband and wife were staying in the hotel. The man woke up in the middle of the night sensing a presence in the room. He opened his eyes and saw the image of a ghost hovering in the corner of the room near the ceiling. He said that the entity was definitely male and seemed to be very angry. The ghost floated across a corner of the bed and then took up a position in the opposite corner where it stayed for awhile before disappearing. The next morning over coffee, they both started to speak at the same time. The man told his wife to go ahead with what she was about to say. She told him of seeing the ghost and that the ghost was a man who was very angry. The husband was amazed that his wife had seen the same thing he had; he thought she had been sleeping when the event occurred."

Mildred smiled as she answered. "Yes, the story is true. That was the spirit of Harvey Hinkil. And yes, Harvey is an angry spirit. In Harvey's latter years, he caught his wife cheating on him. After he witnessed her adultery she left him, but not before emptying their bank account. That left Harvey in an angry state when he died. That anger followed him into the spirit world. He always has an angry look, but more so when he sees women. He has never hurt anyone in the physical world. Harvey doesn't make his presence known very often. We have all tried to get Harvey to set his anger aside, and most times he does. It is when thoughts of his wife enter his mind that he has trouble controlling his anger, but, all in all, Harvey is harmless."

"Wow," exclaimed Harold. "Will I get to meet Harvey?"

"Sorry, Harold, but Harvey will not talk to you," said Simon.

"Harold, be patient. You will talk to everyone who wants to tell you their story," added Mildred.

Harold was about to ask another question, but could only watch as Simon and Mildred disappeared before his eyes.

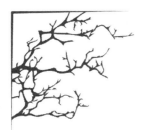

CHAPTER 4

Harold, now in an uplifted mood, walked down the stairs to his room. He copied the file of his interview with Simon and Mildred onto his computer. Then he replayed the interview to make sure that the recorder had recorded everything. Satisfied, he fixed his lunch. He carried a grin of enthusiasm and excitement as he munched down on his sandwich with a glass of red wine.

A thought occurred to him as he finished his lunch. If the ghosts can drain batteries and erase digital pictures and recordings then maybe they could erase the interviews on his computer's hard drive. He spent the next few hours transcribing the audio recordings and when he had finished, he printed out the transcripts. Now, he had a hard copy that could not be erased.

Harold was so engrossed in his work that when he finally finished and looked up, it was almost dark outside. He filed away his printouts and rose from his chair. He stretched and looked around his sitting area. There was a comfortable looking couch on the opposite wall from where he had been working at his table. There was an end table with a Tiffany lamp sitting on top of it at one end of the couch. By the window sat a cozy arm chair. In the window, above the chair, was a heating and air conditioning unit. Curtains covered the rest of the window and hung down to the top of the climate control unit. In the opposite corner, near his table, was a small refrigerator where he had placed some perishables. The microwave that had been sitting on the table, he had moved and placed it on top of the refrigerator in order to provide him maximum workspace. There had also been a coffee pot on his work table which he had placed on the end table next to the couch. Above the table, hanging from the wall, was a fifty inch flat screen TV.

His computer and inkjet printer were also sitting on the table, as well as his audio recorder; his video recording equipment was still in its bag on the floor underneath the table. He had had the bellman bring him a chair so that he could sit at the table to do his work.

With his glass of wine in his hand refilled, he walked into the bedroom. On his right, the bedroom window looked identical to the window in the sitting room with its climate control unit and curtains. On the wall in front of him stood a large armoire where he had hung his clothes. There were also some drawers in the armoire where he had unpacked his suitcase. To his left was the queen sized bed, covered with an Amish quilt and four pillows. On the wall, across from the bed, hung a thirty-two inch flat screen television. Between the armoire and the television was the door that led to the bathroom.

The bathroom had a shower on the left side and a large Jacuzzi hot tub on the right. On the shelf by the sink sat his toiletry articles.

For a fleeting moment, Harold considered stretching out on the couch and turning on the TV. He pulled his mind away from the distraction and left his room to once again meander through the hotel searching for his next interview. The recorder was tucked away in the right front pocket of his sports jacket.

At the elevator he debated whether to take the elevator or the stairs. Finally, he decided to climb the stairs and started his search on the fourth floor. Once again he searched every room before climbing to the fifth floor. Here, while he was walking down the South hallway, he thought he saw an orb of light streaking toward the fire escape door at the end of the hall.

"Wait. Come back. I want to talk to you," he shouted.

Only silence answered his call, so he proceeded to check the rooms one by one, and finding nothing, he climbed the stairs to the sixth floor.

He slowly made his way back to the lobby with no results to show for his efforts, but it had been a fruitful day considering his interview with Simon and Mildred. As he walked down the stairs into the lobby, he saw the nighttime bellman at the front desk talking to the night desk clerk. He was easily recognized by the gold bellman's jacket that he wore.

"Hello Harold," greeted Eric Stone, the nighttime desk clerk. "This is Paul Anderson, one of our nighttime bellmen."

"Hello Harold. It's nice to meet you," smiled Paul.

"Hello gentlemen. How are you two this evening?" Harold asked.

"We're doing just fine," responded Eric. "Since you rented the entire hotel, it is as quiet as it has ever been. How is your research going?"

"Actually, it is going very well," Harold replied. "I suppose you two are probably pretty bored."

"With nobody to check in and out of the hotel," Eric said, "and with no guests around, there is only so much to keep a body occupied. And you can only do so much surfing on the Internet. I forgot to bring in a book to read so it is an especially boring tonight."

"At least I get to go outside once in a while and drive some of the Crescent Hotel guests to downtown restaurants," Paul said.

"I'm thankful Paul is keeping me company when he is not out driving around Crescent guests," added Eric. "Is there anything we can do for you, Harold?"

"No, I'm just making my rounds in search of your permanent unregistered guests."

"I like that," Eric said. "'Permanent Unregistered Guests'. This is your fourth day staying with us. Have you found anything at all?" he asked. Eric was a skeptic and didn't believe the stories about the ghosts, not even those that guests of the Basin Park Hotel had directly told him. He figured they were just making up stories to make themselves more interesting.

"Yes, I have," Harold said. "I've had two interviews already, one on Sunday and one this morning."

Paul, with astonishment written all over his face asked, "You have actually seen ghosts in the hotel?"

"Oh, yes."

"You have been talking to the spirits of the dead and it doesn't bother you?" asked Paul. "I think I would be scared to death if I saw one of them."

"Oh, I don't believe that you have anything to fear from those spirits that reside in the Basin Park Hotel. Some of them may be mischievous, and sometimes they seem to be willing to make their presence known. I find it fascinating to talk to the ones that I have already interviewed, and I find their stories very interesting and enlightening," Harold said.

Astonished, Eric asked, "How many of these things have you seen so far?"

"Three, so far," Harold replied.

"You actually talked to them?" asked Eric doubtingly.

"Oh, yes," Harold replied. "If they're willing, I will talk to them again and hopefully many of the others as well."

"Who are they, and what did they say?" Eric asked, forever the unbeliever.

"Oh. I'm not at liberty to discuss that, but it will all be in the book that I'm writing. Well, gentlemen, I'll see you later. It's time for me to take another tour of the hotel. With any luck I will meet someone else tonight. Hope you don't get too bored." Harold pushed the elevator button; stepped inside and pressed the number six button to once again take him to the top floor.

"I don't know if I want to keep working in a hotel that is haunted," said Paul. "It was one thing not knowing for sure, but now Harold has emphatically declared that the hotel is haunted."

"Oh, come on now," replied Eric. "I don't believe in ghosts. I've never seen anything or heard anything and neither have you."

"No, I've not seen or heard anything."

"So, even if there are spooks in the hotel, they've left us alone. That's all that really counts," said Eric.

"Well, maybe you're right," sighed Paul.

"If there really are ghosts in the hotel, I wouldn't mind if they would come out and keep us company for a while. It would help if we had enough to put a foursome together to play bridge. I have a deck of cards and I'm tired of playing solitaire."

"Oh, you're so funny, Eric," said Paul with a look of concern on his face. Paul's opinion was that he didn't want to have anything to do with any ghost.

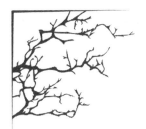

CHAPTER 5

Thursday passed like Wednesday evening. Strange thoughts entered into Harold mind;

Not a creature was stirring, not even a mouse. There would be no clatter on the roof from Santa's reindeer's since Santa had already come and gone. Besides, there was no chimney at the hotel for Santa to come down, except the one in the lobby.

Friday arrived fresh and new, and the snow that had melted on Thursday had come back to cover everything outside once again in a mantle of white. Comfortable and cozy, snuggled up in his bed, Harold had to struggle to make himself get up and move around. While coffee was brewing, he grabbed a quick shower and got dressed. This afternoon at three o'clock the weekend guests of the hotel would be arriving and his work would be postponed until Sunday afternoon. He had checked with the manager, Mr. Rich, and found that there were not enough rooms at the Crescent Hotel to accommodate all of the Basin reservations. Others simply didn't want to move to the Crescent Hotel; they really wanted to stay at the Basin Park Hotel. After a quick breakfast, Harold once again took the elevator to the sixth floor. He looked out the window of the foyer to gaze at the new fallen snow on the ground and wondered how long it would be before it melted away.

By eight o'clock, the housekeepers had started to arrive to clean the rooms that they didn't get a chance to clean on Sunday. The restaurant staff also started to show up to prepare the kitchen for the day's lunch and dinner crowd. A maintenance man had arrived and was walking through the hotel to replace burned out light bulbs and to check for any other possible maintenance issues. The bellman had already unlocked the third and fourth floor smoking balconies. Harold knew that before noon, when the restaurant would open, that the Lucky Seven Bar and Billiard Room would be locked because it would not be open to the public until 6 PM. This was Harold first weekend in the hotel and he was not happy at this interruption, but knew that this was what he had agreed to.

Disenchanted, Harold finished one tour of the hotel and returned to his room. It didn't take long before he began to empathize with those in the lobby, for now he too felt boredom and didn't know what to do with himself. Sunday afternoon seemed so far away. He sat on the couch and stared at the dark screen of the television set.

Then he heard Mildred's voice in his mind saying, "Patience, Harold."

Harold spoke out loud. "Patience. Yes but so hard to practice in the physical realm. How much easier is it to learn patience when you have all of eternity before you?"

In his mind he heard, "You will not be disappointed. The next one you're going to meet is already waiting for you, but not just yet. All things will happen at the appointed time."

For a fleeting moment, Harold could have sworn that he saw Mildred standing in his room wearing her gold dress and a smile, but the image suddenly vanished.

Harold picked up his coat and decided to take a stroll outside, since interviews were impossible with so many people in the hotel. He walked to the elevator and pushed the down button. As the door opened, he saw someone standing in the elevator. "Charlotte," he exclaimed excitedly, but in that moment the vision disappeared. Disappointed, he got off in the lobby and proceeded to take a walk outside. He could tell that the snow would not be on the ground long, for it was melting quickly.

Some of the stores were open and there were not many shoppers/tourists roaming the streets. The sky was still overcast and you could see that the sun was trying to break through. Harold walked up Spring Street and after the Post Office, where Spring Street made a right-hand turn, he turned right, as well. He took note of many of the historic buildings on Spring Street and wondered if any of them were also haunted. Before he realized how far he had gone, Harold found himself in front of the 1886 Crescent Hotel, which was where Spring Street ended. He gazed at the Queen in her Victorian glory as she sat upon the highest mountain in Eureka Springs. With nothing else to do, he decided to take a look at the Grand Old Lady.

As he entered the front doors he saw a large lobby area, much larger than that of the Basin Park Hotel. To his left was the front desk and further along in the left-hand corner was the concierge's desk. Near the middle of the lobby was a huge fireplace. Off in the far right corner sat an old player piano.

"Hello Mr. Sangarius. How are you this afternoon?" asked the general manager, Jason Matthews.

"Mr. Matthews," Harold said with a smile. "I'm doing fine, but since you couldn't move all the Basin guests to the Crescent Hotel, I decided to take a walk around town and wound up here. The Crescent is very beautiful and I like its Victorian charm."

"Mr. Sangarius, anytime that you would like to perform your paranormal investigation at the Crescent, we would look forward to your visit," said Mr. Matthews.

"Maybe someday, Mr. Matthews, but right now my interest is totally focused on the Basin Park Hotel. Many ghost stories have been published about sightings at the Crescent Hotel but I have never seen one about sightings at the Basin. I think that that is the main reason that I'm so interested in the Basin Park Hotel. I've heard stories and seen comments about the Basin ghosts, but nothing in-depth, not like those about the Crescent ghosts. Did your paranormal researchers find anything at the Basin Park Hotel last weekend?"

"Well," Mr. Matthew said, "a few of them said that they had found some minor indications but nothing conclusive. In the years that they have been researching, none have ever found conclusive proof that the Basin Park Hotel is haunted either."

"In that case, my investigation is even more important," Harold said.

"Does that mean that you have found proof that the Basin Park Hotel is haunted?" asked Mr. Matthews.

"I'm sorry, Mr. Matthews, but my investigation is strictly confidential at this point. Anything I find will be written up in my report and then made available to the public when I finish writing my book. You must understand that my investigation and its results belong to the Institute of Paranormal Studies. After all, they are the ones financing this adventure."

"Adventure? Is that how you are describing your research?" asked Mr. Matthews.

"I realize that the word adventure is unusual for this kind of work, but I must say that my investigation has turned into one. Mr. Matthews, please be patient," Harold said. "Patience," echoed through Harold's mind as though Mildred Garfield was near to encourage his own sense of patience.

"I may have to tell the other paranormal researchers that come to the hotel to look upon their research as an adventure. With your ancestral background, I have no doubt that you could find proof positive that the Crescent is really haunted. Again, we would love to have you do an investigation of the Crescent whenever you are ready." Matthews looked at his watch. "Well, Harold, please enjoy your tour of the Crescent Hotel. I hope that your investigation will have much success. I must leave now; I'm late for a meeting."

Harold slowly strolled through the Crescent lobby. Down a short hallway on the left was the Crystal Dining Room, and on the other end of the lobby was the conservatory, a meeting, banquet, and wedding reception room. On the other side of the lobby, across from the front door, was another set of double doors leading out to the patio. Harold climbed the stairs and walked up to each floor. When he reached the fourth floor, he went out onto the balcony which presented an awesome view of Eureka Springs, considering that he was at the highest point in Eureka Springs. Looking out over the balcony, the first site that he saw was the statue of Christ of the Ozarks on the mountain across the valley.

By the time Harold was ready to leave the Crescent, the sun was already setting and it was starting to cool down rapidly. The front desk clerk at the Crescent offered to call the Basin Park Hotel shuttle to take him back to the Basin. Considering that it was getting cold outside, Harold accepted the offer.

Paul was the bellman who picked Harold up in the shuttle, and he asked Harold where he could take him.

"How about taking me to a restaurant called Local Flavor? I hear it is supposed to be very good."

"Yes, the food there is very good. And yes, I can drop you off there. When you finish your dinner you are welcome to call the hotel for a pick up or if you choose you can walk. Local Flavor is only about two blocks from the hotel, but it is getting colder outside so you may prefer to get a shuttle ride back." Harold could tell that Paul desperately wanted to ask him about the ghost activity he had found in the hotel, but he remembered Harold stating that he could not talk about it. They rode in silence for a moment and then Paul pulled up to the curb and said, "Here we are. Local Flavor."

"Thank you," Harold said. "I'll call you when I finish eating dinner."

Harold entered the restaurant as Paul pulled away from the curb and headed back to the Basin Park Hotel.

Harold ordered the prime rib dinner. He took his time enjoying every bite of the meal. And since he didn't expect to have anything to do this evening, he enjoyed two glasses of red wine. An hour later, paying his check and leaving a generous tip, Harold called the Basin Park Hotel and asked to have the shuttle come and pick him up.

Back in his room again, Harold sat on the couch and patted his full belly. There was no point in touring the hotel, since hotel guests were scattered throughout. Harold sat back and contemplated how to spend the rest of his evening. Across on the other wall, the black screen of the TV beckoned to him. He looked down at his computer on the table and then back up to the TV. Finally, he decided to turn on the tube and see if he could find a movie that would be worth watching.

He awoke with a start from dreams of Charlotte and wondering how such a beautiful young woman could be murdered in the prime of her life. The TV was running an infomercial. Harold stretched, rubbed his eyes, and then reached for the remote to turn the TV off. Getting up, he made his way to the bedroom. The nightstand clock said it was three AM, and fleetingly, he considered roaming the hotel while it was now quiet. Instead, he got undressed and crawled into bed hoping to have more dreams of Charlotte.

Saturday morning dawned with sunlight streaming in through the curtains. Harold sat and stretched, disappointed that his dreams of Charlotte had not continued. He got dressed and then walked up Spring Street to a small restaurant, Nibbles, where he had a delicious quiche breakfast. There were quite a few people out on the street; many were window shopping, some stepping inside a store here and there either to shop or just to get out of the morning's chilly air.

With nothing else to do Harold decided to play tourist and wandered the downtown streets. After walking through the downtown area once, however, he decided he didn't need to waste time playing tourist, so he returned to his room and started working on writing his report.

He unlocked the door to Room 317. Stepping inside and after closing the door, he started to make a pot of coffee. He took off his coat and his shoes and put on some slippers. He filled a cup of coffee and sat down at the table. He had his notes and interviews sitting beside his computer. His fingers moved over the keyboard and he started typing his report.

By the time Harold came up for air, it was dark outside. He could feel his stomach complaining in protest at having missed lunch. Harold looked at the clock and found that it was already eight PM; the hotel's restaurant closed at six but others in town would be open until nine. He hurriedly left his room and rushed downstairs and quickly marched to Local Flavor. After devouring his meal, he ordered dessert to go so that he could have a snack later.

Sunday dawned with a cold, sun filled sky that deceived people into believing that it was warmer than it really was. Dreams of Charlotte slowly receded as he stirred from the light entering through the curtained window. Harold went to the restaurant for their buffet breakfast and then returned to his room. It would still be hours before he could start his search again. Sitting in front of his computer, he continued to work on his report but not before setting an alarm for one PM, when everybody should be out of the hotel except for those employees at the front desk.

The ringing of the alarm jolted him from his work. Realizing that it was already once o'clock and his stomach was feeling the discomfort of emptiness, he quickly grabbed something to eat and picked up his recorder before heading out the door and making his way to the sixth floor. Before he left his room, Harold called down to the front desk to make sure that all the doors in the hotel had been unlocked for him.

Excitement filled him now that he was back to his investigation. Harold took his time in each room as he entered the foyer, the Ballroom and then the Lucky Seven Bar and Billiard Room. He spent an hour on the sixth floor before walking down to the fifth floor. He worked his way through the rooms on the south side of the hotel and then proceeded down the main hallway to the north side. As he turned the corner, he thought for a moment that he had seen an orb rushing down the hall. Finding nothing on the fifth floor, Harold walked the stairs down to the fourth floor. He again started checking the rooms on the south side of the hotel and as he entered Room 408, he noticed a definite chill in the room. He lingered there, hoping to have some kind of encounter, but his wait was fruitless. Finding nothing more, Harold climbed down the stairs to the next floor.

This time Harold decided to check the rooms on the north side first and slowly worked his way to the south wing. He especially took his time on this floor because it was considered the most active in the hotel. As he turned down the south hallway he again thought he noticed an orb shooting down the hall toward the fire escape. Then, without a doubt, he saw an orb flash from the room on the right side into one of the rooms on the left side of the hall. He remembered reports from three different guests who didn't know each other and who had been staying in Room 307, Room 309 and Room 310. Each had reported seeing a cowboy walk through their room and each guest reported seeing the apparition at the exact same time. All three of these rooms were on his left hand side and suddenly Harold became very excited. His hopes were resting on an encounter with a cowboy ghost who was believed to be John Chisum. Charlotte had confirmed this rumor, but Harold wanted to meet the old cowboy for himself.

Standing in the hall, he stared into Room 307 for several minutes before entering. This room had two double beds and he sat on one of them, patiently anticipating an appearance. He finally got up and moved to Room 309 where he again waited patiently, sitting on a chair in the corner next to the king size bed. After fifteen minutes, Harold got up and walked to the door of Room 310. He stood outside just looking into the room. Disappointment was already starting to build in him, but once again there was a voice in his head saying "Patience, Harold".

Before he could enter Room 310, he felt a tapping on his shoulder (Harold knew that this was a common thing that happened but he only remembered women reporting being tapped and never a man) and turned to see who was there.

Nothing. He stood there for a long moment before stepping into the room. This room also had two double beds. He sat down in the chair next to the small armoire and patiently waited.

After waiting a long while, Harold became impatient and said to the four walls, "Okay, I have been waiting for a while and you have just been playing with me; first with coldness in Room 408 and then with a tapping on the shoulder while I was standing in front of this room, that is of course not to mention the orbs that have been flying through the halls. If you don't intend to show your-self, I'm going to proceed to the second floor."

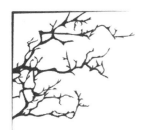

CHAPTER 6

As Harold started to rise from the chair, he heard a voice saying, "Oh my, you can be an impatient one can't you? Mildred did mention that."

Harold sat back down in the chair as he saw a figure appear sitting on the bed across from him. "Well, I only have three weeks left to complete my investigation for The Institute of Paranormal Studies. I'm grateful for them financing my research here at the Basin Park Hotel, but they would only cover the expenses for four weeks. And I really want to interview as many of you as I can."

"Well then, interview away. Oh, and you can turn on your recorder; I promise not to erase your tape."

Harold turned on the tape recorder and began, "What is your name?"

"My name is William Arbuckle the third," the specter said. "Next question."

William Arbuckle the third was a slender man with short cropped graying hair. He was wearing a dark brown suit that seemed, to Harold, to come from the early 20th century. A black top hat, that seemed to be made of beaver pelt, was perched atop his head.

"It sounds like you don't have a lot of patience, either," Harold said.

Laughing, William responded, "You are right. Patience is not one of my virtues."

"You mean to tell me that after all the years you have spent at the Basin Park Hotel you still have not learned patience?"

"I may have all the time in the world now," William said, "but while I was alive I was not a very patient man. I suspect that if you didn't learn patience in the physical realm, that you won't learn patience in the spiritual, either."

"So why is it that you were not a patient man?"

"My business activities were always hectic. My business partners were always expecting me to accomplish more and more. The stress and tension just kept building and I found myself working all the time. Now that I have all of eternity with nothing but time on my hands, I find that patience and tolerance are not easy for me to accomplish."

"What kind of business were you in?" Harold asked.

"I handled the sales and the business of selling notions of one kind or another. My partners handled the manufacturing aspect of the business," replied William.

"What kind of notions did you sell?" Harold asked.

"Well, if you must know, ladies' undergarments." Harold thought that he saw William blushing.

"Did it embarrass you, selling ladies underwear?"

"Yes," was William's one word answer.

"Then why did you do it?"

"Well, there was a lot of money to be made in selling ladies' undergarments. Financially, I did very well," said William.

"But it obviously embarrassed you a lot."

"Do you know how difficult it was to engage in a relationship with a woman once she learned that you sell ladies' undergarments? If you were a woman, how would you feel about talking to a man who knows what you're wearing underneath your outer clothing?"

Harold thought about that for a moment before responding. "Well, I guess it was a lot different back then than it is today. Today you can walk into any department store and find all kinds of ladies' underwear on full display."

"Yes," responded William sourly. "Back in my day, ladies' undergarments were only sold in stores exclusively selling women's clothes. Imagine having to enter one of the stores where ladies entered and here was a man entering their domain to sell them unmentionables. Even the men would look at me strangely, wondering what I was doing going into a woman's store."

"So I take it you didn't have a lot of friends?" Harold asked.

"No," William said. "I couldn't even call my business partners friends. They were just my business partners, and we never had any private associations. Once I was on the road selling our products, the only contact we had was by telegram." answered William.

"It sounds like you had a very lonely life," Harold said.

"Yes. The desk clerks in the hotels were always polite and accommodating. The ladies in the dress shops were not very sociable; all they were interested in was looking through my latest catalog to see if there was anything new that they thought their customers might be interested in." William sighed audibly as he remembered those days.

"Would you consider your life now to be lonely?" Harold asked. "After all, you've spent a lot of time with the people who have come here and decided to stay as permanent residents of the hotel."

William smiled, saying, "Oh, my fellow roommates, or rather hotel mates, are far more understanding now. It wasn't that way in the beginning, but after so many years together they have come to understand the things that I had to endure while alive."

"So, do I understand correctly that you are the one who goes around tapping people on the shoulder?" Harold asked. "You are the one who tapped me on the shoulder, aren't you?"

Laughing, William answered. "Yes. I'm the one."

"I take it you have fun doing this?"

"Oh, yes," grinned William. "I have a lot of fun watching people turn around to see who tapped them on the shoulder. They always have a strange quizzical look on their faces which makes me laugh."

"So, why do you go around tapping people on the shoulder?" Harold asked.

"I suppose that is because when I was alive no one paid me any attention, but now, whenever I tap someone on the shoulder, they all turn around to look at me. It makes me laugh when they see that there is no one behind them."

"Do you do this to get attention?" Harold asked.

"Of course I do. I never got any attention when I was alive, but now everyone that I tap turns around to look at me and even though they can't see me, I love to stay and watch their reaction and to listen to their comments, especially if they are with someone else. In that respect, I'm having more fun now that I'm dead than I ever had when I was alive."

"Do you tap men or women or both?"

"Oh, I tap both, but more often than not it is women that I tap on the shoulder. I find that more exciting and invigorating. The women seem to be more curious about who is tapping their shoulder than the men are. You might understand it better," William chuckled, "if you could witness one of these events, but if you are in the hall at the time, you would be blamed as the instigator. After all, they will be able to see you, but not me."

"Yes, I can see that what you say would be true, even though I would love nothing better than to catch something like that on film," Harold said. "So why is it that you moved into the 1905 Basin Park Hotel and when did you move in?"

"I was staying in the New Orleans Hotel at the time when I died. I didn't die in the hotel, but after death and after the Basin Park Hotel opened in 1905, it seemed the more popular place for my kind to be living. I died on New Year's Eve of 1899."

"If you don't mind my asking, William, what was the cause of your death?" Harold asked.

"I was out celebrating the entrance into the New Year, not to be confused with the new millennium which would happen on New Year's Eve of 1900. I was wandering the streets by myself, going from one bar to another. That was probably my mistake. I was carrying a lot of money on me, and someone must've seen me pull out a lot of cash to pay the bill at one of the bars. I had a lot of $20 gold coins in my pockets, because I was expecting to paint the town red. The more I drank, the more I realized that I had no one to paint the town red with. When I finally decided that I'd had enough to drink, I started wandering back to the New Orleans Hotel. I remember stumbling down the street in a drunken stupor. My brain was in a fog but I kind of remember two men approaching me; they had knives in their hands. I was too drunk to put up any resistance. I felt a knife plunge into my abdomen and then another into my throat. I know I must have died in seconds. The crooks cleaned out my pockets before anyone noticed what was going on. I remember people walking around and stepping over my body and calling me a drunken fool. I guess they must have been pretty drunk as well, considering they didn't notice the blood on the ground. It wasn't until the next morning before the police found my body. I stood over it all listening to the police discussing the situation and concluding that I had indeed been killed and robbed." He gave a wry chuckle. "Ironically, I was killed in front of the Ladies Specialty Emporium."

"Yes," Harold said. "That is ironic considering you did your business there."

"Did you know that when Marty & Elise Roenigk bought the Basin Park Hotel in 1997 that they originally were planning to turn the hotel into a home for seniors?

"Yes I had heard about that."

"None of us were very happy about that. It would have been good for the American senior citizen, but we were already the living dead, most of us cut short in the prime of our lives. Now we were going to have to watch the elderly die here in the hotel, and we've all seen enough death already. We were all glad when the Basin Park stayed a hotel because we can see young lives develop all around us. We really enjoy seeing guests return time after time, because it gives us a sense of living as we see their lives unfold as the years pass by." He winked. "Not to mention, that I really enjoy tapping the young ladies on the shoulder. I just love to see all those pretty young faces turning to look at me. That was something that I had never experienced when I was alive."

With that statement, William Arbuckle the third disappeared in front of Harold's eyes.

Harold sat there thinking about his conversation with William for several minutes before giving up and returning to his room. Excited, he began transcribing the tape. He was not going to take any chances that any of the permanent residents in the hotel would erase the digital recording.

He was so caught up in transcribing William's interview when he unexpectedly felt a tap on his shoulder. Harold jumped up knocking the chair over and as he turned he heard a woman's laugh. Standing in front of him was Mildred Garfield wearing a royal blue hoop skirted dress, her hair piled elegantly upon her head.

"Hello, Mildred," he said. "You surprised the heck out of me."

"I'm sorry I startled you, Harold. Too bad I could not take a video recording of you jumping out of your chair. That was really hilarious," she said.

As Harold's nerves settle down, he said, "You are looking very lovely tonight, Mildred. I admit you really surprised me with that tap on the shoulder. When I turned around I had fully expected to see William Arbuckle the third, since that is what he is famous for."

"When I tell William how you reacted, I'm sure that he would have loved to have been here to witness it." It took Mildred a moment to get her laughter under control.

"To what do I owe the pleasure of your visit?" Harold asked with a smile.

"I came to extend you an invite. We are having a formal dance in the Barefoot Ballroom. We all agreed that we would like you to attend and we have all also agreed to allow you to set up video recording equipment. We all promise you that we will not erase the recording, because we would like you to have a memorial of your adventures here in the Basin Park Hotel." Mildred's smile radiated like a ray of sunshine.

"I would love to join you all for your dance, but I didn't bring any formal wear. I did bring a black suit, however."

"Oh, your black suit will do just fine. I've already seen what it looks like hanging in the closet." She grinned at him.

"Have you been snooping through my room?" Harold smiled at Mildred.

"Nothing inappropriate. I just wanted to be sure that you had something to wear to the dance," responded Mildred.

"In that case, I accept your generous invitation. Of course, I don't think I have ever turned down an invitation from a beautiful lady. And, when is this big event going to occur?"

Mildred giggled. "I suppose you would need to know that detail. The dance is tomorrow night at eight o'clock."

Smiling in delight, Harold answered. "I shall count the minutes."

Harold reached down as if to take Mildred's hand. Mildred, understanding what Harold was about to do raised her hand and Harold then bent forward to kiss the back of Mildred's hand. As he bent forward and gave his kiss, Mildred disappeared from the room.

Excited, Harold picked the chair up off the floor, plopped himself down and continued to transcribe William's interview. In all the excitement he had forgotten about eating dinner until his stomach began complaining for the umpteenth time. He was so thrilled at this opportunity to be a part of the ghostly dances that he had heard about, and to be offered the opportunity to also videotape the dance, that he didn't sleep very well. He dreamed of being at the dance and twirling Charlotte around the room. He pictured Charlotte in a cream colored hoop dress that exposed her milky white, soft shoulders and her beautiful red hair arrayed luxuriously around them. He could feel the softness of her body with his hands around her waist and he could feel the warmth of her hand in his as they danced. He would gaze into her eyes and feel the tension, stress and anxiety being released from his body; he had never felt so at peace. He smiled, feeling like he just wanted to melt away into her very soul.

Harold woke up late the next morning, feeling tired but strangely relaxed. It took him a while to get his mind to comprehend that he had only been dreaming. Reality was waking him up, but at the same time he would have preferred to stay in his dream; it seemed so real and inviting.

After a quick bowl of Cheerios, he jumped in the shower and then got dressed. He picked up his video equipment and took the elevator to the sixth floor. He set his equipment on the raised platform in the Barefoot Ballroom and carefully studied the dance floor to determine where best to place the cameras. After a while he made his way to the lobby and asked the front desk clerk and bellman if he could borrow a ladder. The bellman retrieved a ladder from the first floor, and Harold, with a grin from ear to ear, took the ladder upstairs and proceeded to hang three cameras from the ceiling in the ballroom and hung one camera in the foyer, pointing toward the doors to the ballroom. Next he ran a short test video of all the cameras to make sure that they were aimed where he wanted them. Each camera had a remote control device so he didn't have to worry about manually starting each one. After returning the ladder to the bellman, Harold went back to his room and anxiously waited for the time when the dance would begin. Finally at five o'clock that afternoon he decided he should take a nap before the evening's excitement began. He set a timer for ninety minutes and was soon fast asleep with dreams of Charlotte dancing in his arms. Their lips were about to meet just as the alarm rang.

Harold shot up into a sitting position, dazed and confounded by his surroundings. He fully expected to be in the ballroom as he frantically looked around the room for Charlotte. The ringing of the alarm finally pierced through his bewilderment. He reached over and turned it off, then stumbled to the bathroom and splashed his face with cold water.

He shuffled his way into the sitting room where he grabbed a TV dinner from the freezer and moved it into the microwave oven. He started a pot of coffee and then plopped himself down on the couch. Seemingly disoriented, he sat there with visions of Charlotte still filling his head. He didn't hear the coffee pot as it gurgled at the end of its brewing cycle. It was finally the ding of the microwave oven telling him that his dinner was cooked that finally got his attention. Listlessly he ate the food and washed it down with coffee. Finally, realizing he was going to see Charlotte very soon, he got up and got dressed in a white shirt and his black suit. By 7:30 he was on the elevator on his way to the ballroom. He wanted to be there before any of the guests arrived.

Stepping off the elevator, Harold surveyed the foyer and found it empty. He opened up the ballroom doors and looked around and again he didn't see anyone. He sat down on the raised platform in the ballroom. He took several deep breaths and attempted to patiently wait for everyone to arrive, but in his mind he was truly only waiting for Charlotte.

"Patience, Harold." Once again, Harold heard Mildred's voice in his mind. He quickly looked around expecting to find Mildred watching him. Looking around he still didn't see anyone and he began to wonder how Mildred could get into his head with her constant advice of patience.

Ten minutes before eight, Harold decided to start the cameras. He walked around to all four cameras, pressing the record button on each of the remotes. Then he went back and sat down on the raised platform again and waited. Not five minutes later he heard music filling the ballroom. He saw no one in front of him in the ballroom, so he turned and looked at the stage. His eyes opened in wonder and his jaw dropped open as he watched a full band tuning up and preparing their musical instruments for the evening's entertainment. All the musicians were dressed to the hilt in formal wear. He continued to stare at them until he heard voices behind him. He quickly turned hoping to see Charlotte but what he found was a room full of people chattering away, just waiting for the band to begin playing.

Harold meandered through the room looking for Charlotte. Every one of the permanent residents greeted him by name; they all knew who he was. There was a lot of excitement, enthusiasm and energy in the air. In the distance he saw Simon and Mildred Garfield and started to make his way toward them, but just then the band started on their first musical score and the dancing began in earnest. Simon and Mildred quickly flowed around the room laughing and smiling at one another. Everyone could see that they were deeply in love with each other.

Slowly, Harold maneuvered between the dancers toward the wall. He started wondering why he was being so careful to avoid the dancers when he could just as easily pass right through them. From here he walked to the ballroom entrance. He scanned the ballroom one more time before turning to look into the foyer. He could still not find Charlotte anywhere. And then like magic she was standing there in front of him, a vision of ultimate beauty. His eyes grew large and his mouth fell open and he stared at this vision that had been haunting his dreams. Charlotte was wearing a cream colored hoop dress that exposed her milky white, soft shoulders and her beautiful red hair arrayed luxuriously around them, just as he had seen her in his dreams.

"Good evening, Harold," smiled Charlotte.

"Good evening Charlotte," Harold replied. "You do look exceptionally lovely tonight."

"Why, thank you Harold. Have you been waiting for me?" asked Charlotte with a twinkle in her eye. "I always try to be fashionably late. I always seem to get more attention that way."

"Well, Charlotte, you have all my attention tonight. I don't believe that I have ever seen any woman look as beautiful as you."

Smiling, Charlotte leaned toward him and said softly, "Harold, I have saved this dance for you."

"I so look forward to dancing with you," Harold said, "but how can I hold you in my arms to dance when you are spirit and not flesh and blood?"

"Oh, Harold, my dear, did you not feel William or Mildred tapping you on the shoulder? If you can feel them tapping you on the shoulder, you will be able to feel me when you put your arms around me." With that, Charlotte put one hand on his left shoulder and took his hand in her other.

Harold felt the soft touch of Charlotte's hand on his shoulder and the warmth of her other hand in his. He could feel the warmth of her body reaching out to his as they danced, his eyes never leaving hers and hers never leaving his. He felt as if they were the only two in the room. Unaware that the music had ended, he continued to waltz Charlotte around the room until he heard a sweet soft voice saying, "Harold, the music has stopped. Don't you think that we should wait for the next song?" Charlotte's smile was a radiant glow.

"Oh. I was so enjoying our dance that I didn't hear the music stop. You are such a wonderful dancer that I just didn't want it to end."

"My dear Harold, you're the only one on my dance card tonight. All my dances belong to you."

"I'm truly honored and blessed," Harold said as the music started up again. They danced around the floor time and time again, oblivious to everything. Harold saw no one else but had eyes only for Charlotte. Many of the dancers stood smiling along the wall as they watched Harold and Charlotte dancing with eyes only for each other. Everyone was commenting about Harold and

Charlotte and how good they looked dancing together. At midnight the call came from the bandstand that this was the last dance. Harold didn't really hear the announcement as he took Charlotte in his arms once more. For Harold time seemed to stand still and he felt as if he were in heaven.

The music finally came to an end but Harold was dancing to his own music, lost in heavenly bliss. For Harold and Charlotte, the dance was not over even though everyone else had disappeared except for Simon and Mildred, who stood near the stage and watched with smiles stretching from ear to ear. Simon looked at Mildred and Mildred looked at Simon and then they too continued to dance.

William Arbuckle the third had decided to wander back to the ballroom. It was 2 o'clock in the morning and he was amazed to find Harold and Charlotte still dancing, and Simon and Mildred still dancing with them. He looked at Harold and saw pure love in his eyes and William wondered what that would have been like. In his short lifetime in the flesh he had never experienced love. Even though sadness came upon him as he remembered his physical life, he had a broad smile on his face as he watched Harold and Charlotte. He looked over at Simon and Mildred and saw the same kind of love in their eyes. That caused him to look at Charlotte again. He was nowhere near an expert, only a novice when it came to love, but he was willing to bet his last dollar that Charlotte was in love with Harold. William wondered, "Can one really find love after death? Can a physical being actually fall in love with a spirit being, and can a spirit being really fall in love with someone in the physical realm?" The answer to his question was right there in the ballroom.

Suddenly William felt a presence standing next to him. He turned and saw the cowboy, John Chisum.

"They make a lovely couple, don't they?" John asked, though it was not really a question. John was making a statement and the proof was right there in front of them.

William replied, "Which couple?"

"Both couples, but it is so nice to see that Charlotte has finally found someone that truly loves her, and whom she loves in return," responded John.

"I must say that Harold will be disappointed not to have seen you and talked to you at the dance. He has been so looking forward to meeting you."

"Harold will meet me," said John. "But tonight — tonight was for Harold and Charlotte." John smiled as he disappeared.

The hours rolled by and everyone in the ballroom was oblivious to the snow that was falling. Simon and Mildred had eyes only for each other, but now and then they would look over to Harold and Charlotte. Happiness filled their eyes as they watched the couple dancing.

It seemed that Harold and Charlotte were talking to each other through their eyes but finally Charlotte spoke and said, "Harold, do you realize that it is 5 o'clock in the morning?"

"Oh," cried Harold. "I have kept you up all night and here you are missing your beauty sleep."

Charlotte laughed, "Did you forget that I'm a ghost? We don't sleep, but it is you who needs to sleep. I have so enjoyed spending this evening with you that time didn't seem to exist."

Harold continued to look into Charlotte's eyes, "You are right. Time didn't seem to exist tonight. And frankly, I don't want our time together to end."

"Time really has no meaning for me," said Charlotte. "But time is important for you and the physical world. It has really been selfish of me to keep you up so late."

"It wasn't selfish of you at all. Wild horses could not have dragged me from your side, and I really don't want to leave you now."

"Harold, for you sleep is like breathing. You need both to stay alive."

"Of course, you are right. I didn't feel the least bit tired while we were dancing but now that we have stopped, I'm feeling a little weary. Would you give me the pleasure of escorting me to my room?" Harold asked.

"It would be my honor," smiled Charlotte. They held hands as they walked to the elevator, on the elevator ride to the third floor and as they walked down the hall to stop in front of Room 317. Harold turned to Charlotte and became lost as he gazed into her eyes. He put his arms around her waist and could feel her body as he pulled her close, closed his eyes and kissed her.

He felt Charlotte responding to his kiss and he could feel the warmth and the softness of her lips on his. He could feel Charlotte's arms around him. It was an embrace he didn't want to end but Charlotte finally broke the kiss and said, "Harold, my dear, it is time for you to get some sleep."

"Will I see you again?" Harold asked with worry in his voice.

"Yes," she said, "you most certainly will, but I cannot monopolize your time because you have others to interview. Your research and investigation are important to you and they are also important to us. When you publish your report, people will hopefully have a different impression of the spirit world, and not think of us all as being poltergeists. Now, good night, my dear Harold, and pleasant dreams," answered Charlotte as she took a step back and blew him a kiss before she disappeared.

In a trance, Harold entered his room, got ready for bed and lay down. No sooner had he closed his eyes than he was fast asleep. Dreams of Charlotte filled him and the feel of her caress and her kiss became etched in his mind. The thought of the heat of her body kept him warm through the night and he lost himself in the depths of her eyes.

It was noon before he finally awoke. He could hear Charlotte's voice reminding him that he had more of the permanent residents of the Basin Park Hotel to find and interview.

Harold forced himself to get out of bed and get ready to leave his room. He first went up to the ballroom and retrieved his cameras and brought them back to his room, where he copied the videos onto his computer hard drive. Then, he took one of the cameras and placed it in the main hallway of the third floor pointing down the park side hallway. His hopes were that he might catch a display of orbs dancing in the hall. Then, returning to his room, he grabbed his voice recorder and proceeded to roam the hotel hoping to find someone else to interview. He only had two and a half weeks left to finish his assignment.

As attentive as he wanted to be, thoughts of Charlotte would not leave him. The thought of leaving and returning to Salem, Massachusetts, was weighing heavily on his mind. He started thinking that he was wasting his time roaming the hotel over and over again looking for someone to interview when he would much rather be spending that time with Charlotte.

The rest of the day passed uneventfully. Harold retrieved the memory card from the camera on the third floor and replaced it with a new one and set the camera to record again. Disillusioned and disappointed, Harold finally fixed himself something to eat. He then sat down to watch one of the videos of last night's ballroom dance, focusing on watching himself with the beautiful redhead. As he watched, his thoughts were consumed with that night of ecstasy. Crestfallen that he had not seen Charlotte that day, he lingered until his eyes grew weary and he crawled into bed. Still, happiness filled his dreams with Charlotte by his side throughout the night.

Wednesday arrived but Harold's depression continued. Between tours of the hotel, he decided to watch the third floor videos. That didn't help his mood any, however, because nothing appeared. Even as his stomach growled over and over, thoughts of eating didn't appeal to him. Again that night Charlotte filled his dreams. This time she was wearing an elegant red dress that matched the color and luster of her hair. Her smile never faded and the sparkle in her eyes never left.

He got up bright and early Thursday morning and forced himself to eat breakfast. As thoughts of Charlotte danced in his head, he began his first tour of the day starting again on the sixth floor. Slowly he worked his way through the fifth floor and then down to the fourth. As he started to enter Room 408 he experienced an unexpected chill even out in the hallway.

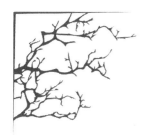

CHAPTER 7

Harold cautiously stepped into Room 408, expecting to see icicles dangling from the ceiling. It was so cold he wished that he had brought a coat with him. The cold seemed to be isolated to this room. He carefully looked around the sitting room before making his way to the bedroom, hoping that it wouldn't be even colder in there. As he opened the door into the bedroom he saw a middle-aged man sitting on the bed. His hair was salt and pepper but leaning more to the salt side. He wore an old coat that had seen better days.

"Come in, come in. I have been waiting for you," the figure said.

"Hello," Harold replied. "You must be Wilbur."

"Yes. I know Simon and Mildred talked about me."

"You do like the cold, don't you, Wilbur?" Harold asked.

"Yes I do. It always brings back memories of that special time of year."

"So you consider winter a special time of year?" Harold started to shiver.

"Oh no. I mean Christmas. It is the most special time of the year."

"Yes," Harold agreed. "Christmas is a very special time of every year."

"I just love the decorations and all the colored lights. Then there is all the joyous music of the season that will lighten anybody's heart. It is a special time when love is in the air and the spirit of giving is everywhere."

"But Christmas has already come and gone," Harold said.

"Ah, but don't you think it should be Christmas all year long?" asked Wilbur.

"That would be a wonderful thing, but it is like two different worlds. For eleven months of the year it disappears. Kind of like your world and my world. The two don't seem to be able to exist at the same time."

Wilbur cocked his head slightly and looked at Harold, who seemed sad. "Why so glum, Harold?" he asked, but then he snapped his fingers and grinned. "Oh, I know. I'll bet it has to do with our beautiful redhead, Charlotte," he said with a wink.

"Is it that obvious?" Harold asked.

"That you are in love with Charlotte?" Wilbur asked. "Yes, it was certainly quite obvious at the dance. Neither one of you could hide your affections for one another." His eyes twinkled.

"Wilbur, do you mind standing up so that I can wrap the blanket from the bed around me. It's pretty cold in here."

Shivering, Harold wrapped the blanket around his shoulders and then sat on the bed beside Wilbur.

"Oh, fine, I will turn off the cold. Charlotte would never forgive me if you caught pneumonia."

"You're probably wondering how I could be so stupid, aren't you? I mean, how can there be a merger of the physical world and the spiritual world other than what I have experienced here in the Basin Park Hotel?"

Wilbur rolled his eyes. "How many times has Mildred told you to be patient? Just as you have to be patient as we present ourselves to you to be interviewed, so also you need to be patient when it comes to affairs of the heart. All good things come to those who are patient enough to wait for them." Wilbur said, smiling. "But right now you have a job to do, to interview me."

Harold smiled and said, "Yes, Charlotte reminded me of it Monday night or rather early Tuesday morning. She told me that she cannot monopolize my time because I have others to interview, and that my research and investigation are important to all of you. She said that when I publish my report that people would hopefully have a different impression of the spirit world and not think of you all as being poltergeists."

"Exactly," he said.

"So, I suppose we should get on with the interview," Harold said as he turned on his recorder. "I know that you like to turn rooms to ice cold freezers. The only stories I have heard of came from people who have stayed in Room 408. Are there any other rooms that you do this to?"

"I do this in other rooms as well, but I particularly like doing it in this room."

"Why particularly Room 408?" Harold asked.

"Oh, there's just something special about this room. I usually only chill down the bedroom, but today I chilled out the sitting room as well, hoping that the cold would attract your attention and that you would come in to see me. It is starting to get warmer and soon you will be able to take off the blanket that you have wrapped around your shoulders." He settled back a bit and smiled. "I remember this one time, when the night time bellman was doing his room checks, turning off the lights, fans and the climate control units. He had just checked the bathroom and the bedroom. As he entered the sitting room, I slammed the bedroom door shut. The bellman jumped as the door slammed shut. He struggled to open the door but I held it shut for awhile before letting him open the door; you see, I wanted a little time to chill down the room before he came back into the bedroom." He laughed delightedly. "Oh, the look on that bellman's face was worth its weight in gold. He could not get out of the room quick enough. I laughed for a long time." Wilber laughed out loud as he remembered the encounter.

"Do you really think that causing the room to be cold will bring the Christmas spirit to the people renting this room?" Harold asked.

"There was a time when I thought just that, but when the room was cold the occupants just turn up the heater. One consolation is that on those nights the people snuggled closer together under the blankets and then feelings of love were certainly in the air." He waggled his eyebrows meaningfully.

"So what prompted you to do these things?" Harold asked.

"Well, when I was alive I worked in an ice factory. It was always cold as we cut the huge blocks of ice into smaller blocks in order to deliver them to people's homes. That was in the days when people had ice boxes, before the invention of the refrigerator. I suppose you might say that I got used to the cold, and I eventually loathed the coming of the hot, humid summer days. I actually feel quite comfortable once I put a chill in the air and it makes me feel physically alive even though I'm dead."

"If you like the ice so much, why don't you find yourself a block of ice and build an ice sculpture to sit on in front of the hotel or in the Basin Spring Park for everyone to see?" Harold asked.

"Oh, I don't do ice sculptures. We only cut huge blocks into smaller blocks to deliver to people's homes during the days when the icebox actually contained a block of ice, but ice boxes were not around for a very long time. Sometimes they even had me delivering the ice to people's homes and I remember the smiles on people's faces as they invited me into their homes to place the blocks of ice into their iceboxes. The pay was not much, enough to live on, but I enjoyed the work most when I was doing deliveries. The people were always happy to see me."

"So where was this icehouse?" Harold asked.

"It was on North Main St. It is the building just south of the Eureka Springs Railroad depot. It used to be called the Ice Factory and Electric Light Plant of Eureka Springs. In 1904 it became the Citizens Electric Company. The building is now deserted and in ruins. It sits as a hollow shell and no one seems to want to restore this historic building back to its former glory. Of course, today, with modern electricity and refrigerators, there is no need for an ice house."

"So how long have you been living in Eureka Springs?" Harold asked.

"Actually, I'm a Eureka Springs native," Wilbur said proudly. "My parents had moved here for the healing springs and they never left. I was born here in a house on Hillside Avenue not far from where the icehouse was. We lived just a few houses down from the Roundhouse which was across the street from the icehouse. The Roundhouse used to be a water storage tank. Now the Roundhouse was turned into a bed-and-breakfast and I'm thankful that this old building has been restored and put to good use."

"And what brought you to the 1905 Basin Park Hotel?"

"I was born in 1867 just after the end of Lincoln's war of Northern aggression. As a youngster I watched them build the Perry House and as a young adult I watched it burn to the ground. It was in 1890 when I started working at the icehouse. That was the same year that the Perry House burnt down. Five years later I married my high school sweetheart, Mary Jane Olson. We had three children, two boys and one girl when the accident happened at the icehouse. There was an electrical failure and you know the icehouse is coated in water, both liquid and frozen. And as you know, water is a really good conductor of electricity. Somehow, one of the power lines fell to the floor. All my coworkers were already on their way to deliver their ice and if the accident had happened just two minutes later, I would still have been alive. I had one more block of ice to load on my wagon and I was just fixing to start up the stairs when suddenly I was jolted by an electrical charge. It felt like my whole body was on fire." His face took on a look of sadness. "I remember falling to the floor and thought I had just passed out, but the next thing I knew I was staring down at my body. I didn't feel any physical pain at this point, but the emotional pain of never holding my wife or my children in my arms again was unbearable. I thank God that the Citizens Electric Company provided some relief for my family after I was gone. I watched the agony on the faces of Mary Jane and the children as they had to face a life without their husband and father. They were so distraught that two months later they moved out of town. I had stayed with them during that time, but when they left I felt even more isolated and alone. Then I heard that other spirits were taking up residence in the 1905 Basin Park Hotel. So I decided to move in here where at least I would have the company of others of my kind."

Harold watched Wilbur's face contort in agony as he relived the moments of that tragic time.

"I don't recall any stories from Basin guests that reported ever seeing you," Harold said as he tried to draw Wilbur's mind away from his heartbreaking past.

"That is because I have never allowed anyone in the physical world to see me. I just have fun watching people's faces as I turn their warm comfortable room into a cold and uninviting place. I laugh when people rush to check the heating/air-conditioning unit or when they call to the front desk complaining about the temperature."

"You certainly do have a way of getting people's attention," laughed Harold. "And I thank you for taking away the cold and warming up the room." Harold removed the blanket and spread it back onto the bed. "What were the names of your children?"

"Falon was the name of the oldest. We named our second son Roy. Our daughter was the youngest and we named her Angel. Even as a baby she was so very beautiful, and for a few years at least I saw her blossom. Unfortunately, I have not seen any of them since they moved out of Eureka Springs." A resigned sadness filled Wilbur's voice.

With that, Wilbur faded away and Harold found himself alone. He turned off his recorder, returned to his room and began transcribing his interview with Wilbur. When he finished, he sat down on the couch and stared into nothing as his mind wandered between Charlotte and fixing dinner. His stomach had been complaining most of the day but the thought of eating just didn't appeal to him.

"DO YOU REALLY THINK we should be spying on Harold this way?" asked Mildred while she and Simon were watching Harold as he sat on the couch.

"Were not spying," said Simon. "We are protecting Charlotte. After all, you can see that she is very much in love with Harold."

"Yes and we can see that Harold is deeply in love with Charlotte," sighed Mildred. "But he is of the physical world and we are of the spirit world. Can there really be a union between the two?"

Simon answered. "I think love can transcend time and space and even these two separate worlds of ours. You saw it for yourself during the dance. The depth of their love for each other was evident in their eyes."

As Harold's eyes blurred the vision of the physical objects in front of him, Simon and Mildred Garfield suddenly appeared standing in front of him. Their faces were lit up with smiles.

No matter what world you are in, smiles are always contagious and a suddenly smiling Harold greeted them, "Hello Simon and Mildred. I wasn't expecting to see you."

Mildred laughed. "It's nice to see you too."

Simon smiled as he said, "At least our appearance has got you to smile. We were tired of seeing that frown on your face."

"I always enjoy visiting with both of you. I just love the way you are both always so happy and obviously very much in love. It is a joy to behold that love isn't restricted to the physical world."

Simon and Mildred looked lovingly into each other's eyes before Mildred spoke. "And is it not wonderful that love can transcend both the physical and the spiritual world?"

"Can it really?" Harold wondered aloud.

Simon answered. "We are all witnesses to that very fact."

"Harold," said Mildred, "the weekend is approaching and tomorrow the hotel will be filled with guests again. You must keep up your strength, so even though we know the thought of eating does not appeal to you, you must eat to keep yourself healthy."

"I know," Harold sighed, answering Mildred as he looked upon her as with the eyes of a child toward his mother. He felt a bond with Mildred that did seem quite motherly. He longingly looked at her, hoping that she had the answers to the questions that were racing through his mind.

"What are your plans for the weekend, Harold?" Simon interjected after a long moment of silence.

"I think I'm just going to spend the weekend in my room. I don't feel like dealing with people right now... Oh, I don't mean you. I mean people from the physical world. I do enjoy our visits and actually all the visits I have had, and I do look forward to meeting more of the Basin Park Hotel's permanent residents."

Harold glanced at his wristwatch then said, "It's almost eight o'clock and if I'm going to eat dinner, I'm going to have to leave now. Local Flavor closes at nine. I really do hate cutting our visit short."

"Take your coat and go enjoy your dinner. We will be visiting again," Mildred said with a twinkle in her eye.

Harold left the room with Simon and Mildred still standing where he could see them. As he closed the door he caught a glimpse of Simon taking Mildred in his arms and kissing her passionately. As he stepped out of the hotel, he turned up the collar of his coat. A cold wind was blowing and snow was falling as he carefully and quickly made his way to Local Flavor.

Back in Harold's room, Simon had left. Mildred walked into the bedroom to find Charlotte sitting on the bed. Charlotte's ever present smile had been replaced by a frightful look of loss and disappointment.

"What are you so gloomy about?" asked Mildred.

"When I was alive," she said, "I didn't know true love. Oh, I loved my husband in my own way, but I love Harold so much more. How can it ever be when we live in two separate worlds? You and Simon were truly in love in the physical world and here you are truly in love even in the spiritual world. Why is it that I have found true love in death, but couldn't find this kind of love in life?"

"I understand how you feel but don't dwell on the future. We have all of time before us. You need to enjoy this moment and embrace it. Forever you will remember the precious time you and Harold spent together. And I'd say that it is quite obvious that Harold truly loves you, too."

"I know that Harold loves me. I can see it in his eyes when he looks at me, and I can feel it when he holds me in his arms, but he will be leaving in just two weeks. Then he will be back among the living. When he is among his own kind, I'm sure he will soon forget me." Ghostly tears were starting to stream down Charlotte's cheeks.

"I seriously doubt that Harold will ever forget you, Charlotte. I have seen the way he looks at you, and I've seen the sparkle in his eyes and yours. No man could love a woman more than Harold loves you; all the more reason for you to enjoy and embrace these next two weeks. Right now, he is just as depressed as you are. Don't let him see how unhappy you are. Smile and laugh and fill these next two weeks with the happiness and enchantment that you both deserve. You do know that you have been in his dreams ever since the day he met you?"

"No, I was not aware of that," smiled Charlotte. "Still, I cannot give him what his physical life deserves."

"Only Harold has control of his physical life. Only he can decide for himself what will be in his tomorrows. None of us, in the physical realm or the spiritual realm, have any control of the future. You must enjoy the present, and your present for the next two weeks should be with Harold."

"You're right. There is no controlling the future. And you're right, I do have the present that I can spend with Harold, and I will always have the time we spent together in my memories."

"It makes me so happy to see you smiling again. I will leave you now, for you have an entire weekend to embrace and to share your love," said Mildred as she disappeared.

As Harold returned from dinner, he found Charlotte sitting on the couch. She stood up as he entered and closed the door. As they embraced, Harold could feel the warmth of Charlotte's body and the gentle loving touch of her arms around him. Their lips melted together as he felt the pressure of her lips on his. There was no thought in his mind that Charlotte was a being of spirit and not of flesh; the embrace and the kiss were so real. Time seemed to stand still for both of them. When they finally parted, Harold took Charlotte's hand in his and they sat on the couch, staring into each other's eyes and enjoying talking and just being with each other.

When Harold started to yawn, Charlotte said, "I think it is bedtime."

"I'm tired," Harold replied, "but I don't want you to leave my side."

"I won't," said Charlotte. "I will be lying right next to you."

Harold beamed with joy as he went to the bedroom and got ready. As he climbed into the bed, Charlotte was already lying under the covers. Lying down, Charlotte rolled into his arms. She felt so real and alive. He fell asleep with a sense of overwhelming happiness that he had never known.

He woke up late Friday morning and was so thrilled to find Charlotte still nestled in his arms. He realized that this was the love that he had been looking for but had never found. Those thoughts brought him joy and sadness at the same time. Joy because the woman of his dreams was lying in his arms and sadness because he would have to leave in two weeks.

Charlotte sensed that Harold was awake. She leaned over and gave him a passionate good morning kiss, "Good morning, my love. I hope you slept well."

Harold grinned, "I do believe that that was the best night's sleep I've ever had in my life. Holding you in my arms and feeling the warmth and softness of your body was so comforting. And being greeted in the morning with a kiss like that, well, it was the most wondrous thing I have ever experienced. How did you sleep?"

Charlotte laughed, "Have you forgotten that I'm of spirit?"

"Yes, I guess I did. You may be a spirit being, but you are real to me."

"Well my darling, it is time for you to get some breakfast. I understand that Nibbles serves an excellent nutritious breakfast."

"I don't really want to think about food. I just want to spend every moment with you," Harold replied.

"You must keep up your strength. I don't want to see you get sick, so please go and have breakfast for my sake."

"Will you come with me?" Harold asked.

"Absolutely. I don't want to leave your side." She reached out and touched his face. "I love you so very much, more than I dreamed would be possible."

There were a few people out on the street but everyone turned their head to look at Harold as he seemed to be talking to himself. What they couldn't see was Charlotte, with her arm in his, walking beside him. They talked while he ate breakfast. The only other two people in the restaurant stared at him thinking that he had lost his mind. It was strange to hear a person talking, then pausing and then talking again as if he were having a conversation with someone who was not there.

They spent the day together in Harold's room, talking, embracing and taking time out for long passionate kisses. The weekend passed with them never leaving each others side until Charlotte commented that it was now Sunday and all the guests and employees had left the hotel. She reminded him that he still had his work to do and others were waiting to be interviewed by him.

"We cannot be remiss in our duties," she said. "You have work that you must do, but I will be waiting here for you. Before you leave, I would ask you if you would mind turning on the video of our dance in the ballroom. I would enjoy reliving that moment over again."

They embraced and kissed before Harold turned on the video. He picked up his recorder and opened the door. He looked back one more time to see the luster of love shining full force from Charlotte's eyes. Reluctantly he closed the door.

He hurriedly made his way throughout the hotel anxious to return to the love of his life. Suddenly he heard a voice, "Harold what are you doing? How many times has Mildred admonished you to be patient. Charlotte is waiting for you, have no fear."

Turning toward the voice, Harold saw Simon standing behind him.

Smiling, Simon said, "I know what it is like to be in love. I feel about Mildred the way you feel about Charlotte. She is in your room waiting for you. She knows that you must do your work, just as all wives know that their husbands have to go to work, too. She will be waiting for you when your work for the day is done. She knows that there are others that want to talk to you and she will not deprive them of that opportunity. And just like any job, you can not just rush through the day and expect to do a good job."

"Yes, I know. It's just that I miss her so when we're part."

"Of course you do. That is part of what love is all about. Mildred and I felt the same way during our physical lives. When I left to go to work in the morning, I was always anxious to be home with her again. In a way we are fortunate that, in death, we can spend all our time together. Coming home from work made it extra special for us to be together again. Certainly you don't want to deprive Charlotte of the joy that she will have when you publish your work."

"No, I wouldn't want to do that. Making her happy is my only desire."

"Then, you must do what every man must do, and do your work diligently."

"I will," Harold said as he pushed the up button for the elevator.

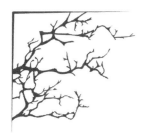

CHAPTER 8

Admonished, this time Harold took his time as he went searching for his next visitor. As he started down the north hallway of the fifth floor he did a double take just as he was leaving Room 519. He thought he had seen something in the door and when he turned to look he was sure that it was a lion. Standing and gazing at the door he remembered that there was a story about a priest and a lion in Room 519.

Harold went back into the room and as he looked into the bedroom he saw a priest sitting in one of the chairs. His hair was gray and neatly combed. He was wearing the typical Catholic priest's black gown.

"Hello," exclaimed Harold.

"Hello Harold," spoke the priest. "I must have just missed you when you were in the room. I'm glad you came back."

"It was the lion in the door that caught my attention."

"Oh, that was Leo."

"Leo?"

"Are not all lions named Leo?" asked the priest with a chuckle.

"I don't think so. I remember seeing a movie with Tony Randall and a lion. That lion's name was Fluffy," Harold replied.

"I guess you can teach an old priest new tricks," laughed the priest.

"Who are you?" Harold asked.

"I'm Father Daniel. It is very nice to meet you Harold," answered the priest. "We would have met you sooner but Leo didn't want to cooperate. Leo can be pretty stubborn at times."

"So, Father Daniel, how long have you and Leo been here at the 1905 Basin Park Hotel?" Harold asked.

"Oh my, we have been here since the roaring 20's."

"So what happened in the 1920's that brought you and Leo to Eureka Springs?"

"We didn't come to Eureka Springs together, but that was the time when a lot of circuses crisscrossed the country. I was a priest here in Eureka Springs. Actually I was stationed at St. Elizabeth's Church; you know the one that sits just below the 1886 Crescent Hotel."

Bewildered, Harold asked, "So how did you and Leo meet?"

"I'm afraid it was not a very pleasant meeting."

"If you were staying at St. Elizabeth's Church, what were you doing in the Basin Park Hotel?"

"We had a church conference in the hotel and since other priests from around the state were staying at the hotel, I stayed as well. What brought Leo to the hotel is quite a different story."

"So you are telling me that Leo was with the circus?" Harold asked.

"Yes. The circus set up out on Highway 62 eastbound. There was an open field there. Now there was an abandoned old hotel there at Ridgeview Road; its name was the Victoria Hotel. The report had gone out on the radio that Leo had escaped from the circus. I was not aware of it because we were in meetings all day. Somehow, Leo had made his way all the way downtown without anyone seeing him. I'm not sure how he got into the hotel; probably through the back door which was always open for the restaurant staff. And I don't know how he got into my room. After a long day of meetings, I was so thankful to be in my room. As I closed the door, I felt a presence in the room. I never in my life would have expected to find a roaring lion there, but there he was licking his lips, baring his teeth and growling. All I could do was back myself in a corner; I grabbed hold of my crucifix and started praying."

"My goodness, that must have been extremely terrifying," muttered Harold.

"Believe me, it was."

"So what happened?" exclaimed Harold sitting on the edge of the bed in anticipation.

Father Daniel rolled his eyes and grinned. "The obvious happened. As you can see, I died."

"Yes, but that does not explain Leo's spiritual apparitions."

Father Daniel laughed. "There wasn't really anything I could do. Leo attacked and all I had to defend myself was the cross of Christ. As Leo's jaws bit into me, I rammed the cross into his throat. Both wounds were fatal and it is unfortunate to say but death lingered for a long time before it claimed both of us."

"And now you and Leo are friends?" Harold asked.

"Oh, yes. We may have been bitter enemies in life but here in the spirit world where neither one of us can harm each other we have learned to become friends over the years," explained Father Daniel.

"But shouldn't you be in heaven? After all you are a priest," Harold asked.

"Who knows the ways of the Almighty? Only He knows the beginning from the end and only He knows the answers to all our questions. We will all stand before the judgment seat on the Day of the Resurrection of all His creation," answered Father Daniel in his priestly way.

"I'm curious. Generally the hotel guests report seeing the lion in the door but nobody seems to mention seeing you. Why is that?"

"Oh, that is because Leo sometimes likes to recreate his days in show business in the circus. He does not do it often, but sometimes he just looks for attention," Father Daniel said, winking.

"How do the other spiritual guests of the hotel get along with Leo?" Harold asked.

"Everyone gets along just fine; after all, Leo cannot hurt them. He loves for them to pet him and scratch behind his ears," laughed Father Daniel.

"Leo, come here," called Father Daniel. "Let Harold pet you so he can see that you are no longer a ferocious animal."

Suddenly Leo appeared sitting in front of Harold. His tongue was hanging out and he was panting like a dog. Harold reached over and patted him and scratched Leo behind his ear. Leo felt as if he were in animal heaven. Without warning Father Daniel and Leo disappeared.

Harold made his way back to the third floor but before returning to his room he stopped and changed the memory card in the video camera. Then he hurried to his room to transcribe the interview with Father Daniel, yet he felt more excitement about seeing Charlotte.

When he opened the door, he found Charlotte just as excited at seeing him. He told her about his latest interview and after a long embrace and kiss, he sat down in front of his computer and began transcribing his interview with Father Daniel. When he was done, Charlotte insisted that he continue working, looking for another spirit to interview. She offered to review the videos of the third floor park side hallway; that would keep her occupied while he was gone and save him the time of having to review all the tapes himself. Warmly and lovingly they hugged and kissed each other before Harold reluctantly left the room to continue his search.

While Harold was on a search, Mildred popped into Room 317 and stood before Charlotte.

"Oh Mildred, what am I going to do. He is going to leave soon," cried Charlotte. "Why is it that I love more in death than in life?"

Mildred answered. "Charlotte, by now you should have learned patience. What a wonderful gift you have received, for in life you didn't find love, but yet you found love in death and how much more permanent is it now than it would have been then. Is this love not a forever love?"

"Is it possible? Is that at all possible?" wondered Charlotte.

Mildred spoke, "Charlotte, have you forgotten that with love all things are possible? Did you know that Harold has been dreaming about you every night since the two of you met? You two have something extremely special."

"He has been dreaming about me? We cannot control people's dreams." She stood and spun around, wrapping her arms around herself in delight. "How wonderful it is to know that there is someone who thinks about me day and night," smiled Charlotte. "But now I have to return to watching these videos for Harold. He is hoping to catch a light display of orbs."

"And he will get them," replied Mildred, "but you know as well as I, that that will not happen until this Thursday night."

"Yes, I know. I'm excited for Harold to see that."

"Then why are you wasting your time watching these videos when you know there is nothing there?" asked Mildred.

Charlotte giggled like a young girl. "You're right. It is kind of boring just looking down the same hallway when I know that the picture will not change until Thursday night, but Harold is excited that I'm helping him with reviewing these videos." Charlotte beamed as she smiled.

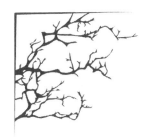

CHAPTER 9

It was Wednesday night of Harold's third week in the hotel. His hopes of having another interview this week were waning. He decided that this was his last tour of the evening. He was ready to spend the rest of the evening with Charlotte. He walked down the stairs to the fifth floor and started his search on the southern wing. He had to force himself to slow down and to be patient. As anxious as he was to be with Charlotte, he knew that she would be there waiting for him no matter how long it took him to make his final tour for the night. Breathing deeply, he slowly and carefully checked the rooms one by one before proceeding down the main hallway and then began the search down the north wing of the floor.

Room 517 - nothing. Room 515 - nothing. Room 514 - nothing. Only Room 512 left to go on this floor, on this wing.

Harold was about to step into the hallway from Room 514 when suddenly he turned back and listened carefully. He thought he had heard a little girl crying. From the sitting room he walked back into the room and checked the bathroom. Finding nothing, he stepped into the bedroom. Nothing, but still he could hear a little girl crying. Bewildered, Harold called out, "Hello, hello? Hello, is there anyone here?"

"Of course there is. Did you not hear me crying?" answered a child's voice.

"There you are," exclaimed Harold. A little girl appeared before him sitting on one of the beds.

The girl wore a light pink colored dress with short ruffled sleeves and the hem of the dress and sleeves were bordered with white lace. Her eyes were a deep blue and tear filled. Her light brown hair was very curly and it reminded Harold of a little movie star girl named Shirley Temple.

"It is my turn," pouted the little girl. "Silvia was trying to take my turn."

"Who is Silvia?" wondered Harold.

"See, you would rather talk to Silvia than to me," pouted the little girl.

"Oh. No, no. I really want to talk to you," insisted Harold.

"No, you don't, you want to talk to Sylvia."

"Silvia is not here," Harold said gently, "so it is your turn."

"How do you know Silvia is not here?" The little girl continued to pout, "You have not even met Silvia yet, so you don't even know what she looks like. She may be here trying to talk to you before I get my turn."

"I promise you that she will not interfere with our meeting," smiled Harold as he watched a ghostly female apparition smiling as she stood behind the girl and then vanished before his eyes.

"Do you really promise? I know adults sometimes say they promise, but they don't always mean it," said the little girl with a hopeful look in her eyes.

"You have my word of honor," Harold replied. With his recorder running, Harold asked, "so, what is your name?"

"I'm Abigail, Abigail Carter."

"And how old are you, Abigail?"

"I'm six years old."

"So how did you come to live in the Basin Park Hotel?" Harold asked.

"I was living in the Southern Hotel just across the park until it burned down on November 12, 1932. That is when I moved into the Basin Park Hotel," answered Abigail.

"So why did you wait so long before moving here? You could have moved here when the Basin Park Hotel opened in 1905?" Harold asked.

"Silly man," giggled Abigail, "the Southern Hotel was my home but when it burned down I had to find myself a new home."

"So how did you come to make the Southern Hotel your home?" continued Harold.

"You are funny. I like you Harold," laughed Abigail. "My mother and father brought me to the Southern Hotel. How else could I get there? I'm only six years old and no one would rent a hotel room to a six-year-old." Abigail was rolling all over the bed unable to contain her laughter.

"That is funny," laughed Harold. Abigail's little child laughter brought joy to his heart. "Do you know why your mother and father came to Eureka Springs with you?"

Abigail continued her giggling, "Silly man. My mother and father didn't come with me to Eureka Springs; they are the ones that brought me to Eureka Springs." Again, Abigail laughed hysterically.

Harold could not help but continue laughing. He realized that he was the one who was asking silly questions. He loved the fact that he had brought some joy into this little girl's heart especially considering that he had just moments ago heard her crying. "Okay. Do you know why your mother and father brought you to Eureka Springs?"

Abigail's laughter subsided as she remembered those days long ago, "My daddy was not feeling very well and mommy had suggested that the healing springs of Eureka Springs might cure him of his ailments."

"It seems that most people, back then, came to Eureka Springs for the healing waters," observed Harold.

"The waters did heal quite a few people, but I don't know if they ever healed my daddy," frowned Abigail.

"Where are you mommy and daddy? Are they here in the Basin Park Hotel with you?"

"I don't know where my mommy and daddy are," said Abigail with tears streaming down her face.

"Are you saying that you have been all alone since you were six years old?" gently Harold asked.

"Yes." It seemed like Abigail was on the verge of bursting out crying again.

"Do you remember what happened that left you all alone?" Harold could only imagine what kind of agony Abigail was going through.

"I remember mommy and daddy telling me to stay in the room. They were going out to bring home some dinner from one of the restaurants on Main Street. They left but never came back. I was very worried about them and was very afraid at having to spend the night alone. I remember crying myself to sleep and praying for God to bring them home to me. When they didn't show up in the morning, I went out looking for them but could not find them. I think I must have searched for hours. I finally went back to my room in the Southern Hotel. I was very hungry and I searched the room for any kind of food but could not find any. I went back outside that afternoon trying to find something to eat and I found a few scraps lying here and there. I even stopped people on the streets asking them for food; they just made snide remarks about beggars and turned and walked away." Her face clouded again.

Harold found himself on the verge of tears as he listened to Abigail's story, "That is a terrible thing for them to turn their backs on a hungry child."

"For two days all I was able to get to eat were scraps that I found lying in the park and in restaurant trash cans. I cried myself to sleep every night. I had even asked all the police officers if they could find my mommy and daddy, but then things got even worse. The hotel staff knew that my mommy and daddy were missing. I walked through the lobby to my room many times. One day when I came back into the lobby after scrounging for food, the man at the desk said they had removed all our things from our room and that I was not allowed back in the hotel until my mommy and daddy returned. My mommy and daddy had paid for the room in advance but they were not around to give the hotel more money to continue renting the room. I was a little upset at the time and started crying. I didn't know what I was going to do. I was six years old. I didn't know how to even really take care of myself. In a way, I could not blame the desk man because my clothes were dirty and my face stained with dirt and it was an elegant hotel and my appearance was not acceptable. They even insisted that I remove all our things out of the hotel. Can you imagine that? A six-year-old girl who could not even lift her own luggage was supposed to cart away her mommy and daddy's suitcases as well?"

With painful, tear filled eyes, Harold asked, "What did you do then?"

"The hotel people carried our luggage and dumped it all in the park. I opened up my suitcase and removed as much as I could so that I would be able to carry what was left. I dragged my case with me wherever I went. I went to the churches but no one would let me in because I was so dirty. I finally found a hole where I could hide my luggage and that is where I slept too. When it got dark, I would go to one of the springs and take a bath. I remembered that my mommy always used soap when she gave me a bath but I didn't have any soap. After I bathed, I put on clean clothes and tried to wash my dirty dress in the spring water but I had no soap to clean them with, either. I was so hungry and I could not get anyone to help me. I lived off crumbs that I found but after a few days I found my stomach was cramping really bad and one morning I just didn't have the energy to get up and go hunting for food. I just stayed in my hidey hole and that is where I died. At some point I found myself standing up and looking down and seeing my body lying there. That is when I realized that I must be dead. I was not hungry anymore and my clothes looked clean and new. I walked through the streets of Eureka Springs and no one seemed to notice me. I was looking all around when I suddenly realized that I had walked through a bench that was sitting in the park. That is when I realized that I was a ghost and no one was able to see me. That is when I decided to move back into the Southern Hotel."

Tears were streaming down Harold's cheeks as he commented, "What happened to you is a terrible thing and should not happen to any little child."

"It's okay now," Abigail tried to reassure Harold." Now, I'm never hungry. I never get dirty so I never have to worry about taking a bath." Abigail started giggling again. "I only cry when I start thinking about my mommy and daddy and what happened to them. And sometimes people in the hotel hear me. I also have a lot of fun with the guests in the hotel. Sometimes I let them see me and I watch the surprised looks on their faces as they wonder whether they really saw a ghost or not.

"I remember this one time when a family was staying in Room 514. It was a mommy and daddy and two little girls. They all heard me crying and came in the bedroom to look for me, but I was standing at the window outside the room. I watched them and when one of the little girls went into the bathroom, I snuck inside the room. As the little girl went to leave the bathroom, I held the doorknob so that she could not get out. I laughed; it was so funny. At least, it was funny until the little girl started to cry; that is when I let the doorknob go. Her tears reminded me of how scared I was when my mommy and daddy disappeared."

"Abigail, thank you very much for sharing your story," expressed Harold sincerely.

"You and Charlotte make a beautiful couple," said Abigail.

Harold grinned. "I suppose all the spirit people in the hotel know about Charlotte and me."

"Oh yes and we are all overjoyed to see you two so happy," smiled Abigail with her little girl smile.

"I suppose you missed our first ballroom dance. I guess you were probably sleeping because it was such a late hour when the dance began."

"Silly man," laughed Abigail. "We spirit people don't need sleep. I was there at the dance."

"I didn't see you there," Harold replied.

"Silly man," Abigail continued to laugh, "You didn't see anybody at the dance. You only had eyes for Charlotte. Funny man."

Harold could hear Abigail's laughter for several minutes after she disappeared from his view. He smiled as he thought about that ballroom dance. "Yes," he said to himself, "I did only have eyes for Charlotte." Even though these thoughts were in his mind, Harold didn't realize that he had vocalized them for all the spirit people of the Basin Park Hotel to hear.

Harold had a big smile on his face as he forgot about continuing the rest of his rounds of the hotel. He quickly returned to his room to transcribe Abigail's interview but he was in just as much of a hurry to hold Charlotte in his arms again.

As Harold entered his room, he slammed the door shut behind him as he rushed into Charlotte's arms and passionately kissed her. "Charlotte, I missed you so much."

"Oh. I like that," laughed Charlotte, "You have not even been gone for an hour, but now it is time for you to transcribe your interview with Abigail."

"You knew I was interviewing Abigail?" asked a surprised Harold.

"Of course I did. We all knew. It's hard for people in the spirit world to keep secrets," smiled Charlotte as Harold watched the stars dancing in Charlotte's eyes. "Now, you need to get busy transcribing and then we will have the rest of the evening together."

Harold sat down in front of his computer and as he started his transcription, he asked Charlotte, "Did you see any activity on the third floor videos?"

"No. There was nothing there. Just an empty hallway, but I'm sure that before you leave you will find what you're looking for." Charlotte smiled behind Harold's back, knowing that tomorrow night he would have the video that he was hoping for. She was content to keep that secret in anticipation of the joy that she would see in Harold's eyes when he watched the orbs putting on a light display down the third floor park side hallway.

Thursday arrived and Harold continued his searches through the hotel. After each round he returned to his room to spend a little time with Charlotte, and each time Charlotte had to encourage him to continue his work. He continued to change the memory card in the video camera pointing down the third floor park side hallway at regular intervals and brought them to Charlotte to review. He was thankful that Charlotte had offered to watch the videos for him so that he didn't have to spend many hours or even days watching to find nothing happening. Little did he realize that Charlotte had no need to watch the videos because she already knew that the display that Harold was looking for would happen that night while he was sleeping. The day passed uneventful and Harold was overjoyed that the weekend had arrived so that he could spend the whole time with this amazing woman.

Friday morning, Charlotte woke Harold from his slumber before seven o'clock so that he could remove the video camera before the employees arrived to begin preparing the hotel for the arrival of their weekend guests.

As Harold dressed himself to prepare to go to breakfast, he saw Charlotte dressed in a pure white gown and wearing a gold colored wool coat that stretched down to her ankles. Her red hair shimmered; her eyes sparkled; her lips curled up with a big smile. Arm in arm they made their way to the lobby. Stepping into the street they watched the sky release a fluttering flow of white that had already covered the streets.

They walked through the snow-covered park on their way to the Gazebo Café at the Best Western's Eureka Inn, right at the intersection of Main Street and Highway 62, so that Harold could get his breakfast. There were only a couple of people out and about at that time of the morning. They stared at Harold as he was talking to Charlotte but all they saw was Harold talking to himself and always glancing to his right as if there was someone there on his arm. Even his arm was crooked as if someone had their arm linked with his. They also noticed that there was only one set of footprints walking through the park.

As Harold was finishing his breakfast, Charlotte suggested, "You may want to order a breakfast to go, something you can put in the refrigerator for tomorrow morning."

"Aren't we going to have breakfast here tomorrow?" Harold asked.

Charlotte laughed, "Oh, I think I forgot to tell you that we will be dancing all night long. The dance is in the ballroom and starts at one o'clock in the morning after the Lucky Seven Bar and Billiard room has closed and everyone has left the sixth floor. So I think you will probably be sleeping through breakfast."

"In that case, by all means I will order a breakfast to go. I can hardly wait for the dance to begin," declared Harold.

"I was sure you would feel that way," smiled Charlotte. "You may want to take a nap this afternoon so that you will be able to dance the night away. I, too, eagerly await this evening's dance. I love the way you sweep me around the dance floor, not to mention sweeping me off my feet."

The few customers in the restaurant also stared at Harold as they watched him in animated conversation as if there was somebody sitting across from him. With astonishment in their eyes they listened as he spoke and then answered an unheard response. They all concluded that Harold was a mental case.

When they finally returned to their room, Charlotte suggested that they watch the video together. She already knew what they were about to see. She had seen it herself, in person, on several occasions. Now she watched Harold's face in anticipation of the excitement which he was about to experience.

Harold started the video and sat down beside Charlotte on the couch and put his arm around her shoulders. They sat there and watched the video and as the light show began, Charlotte watched Harold, whose jaw dropped as he watched in utter astonishment and fascination.

"Oh, my God!" exclaimed Harold. "This is absolutely wonderful. Since you never saw anything on the other recordings, I was sure that I would never see such a spectacular event." He watched as the orbs floated, danced and dashed up and down and around and all over the hallway. It was like watching a musical symphony without the sound. He took a moment to glance at Charlotte and when he looked at her he had to ask her, "Why are you watching me and not the video?"

Charlotte could not contain her laughter, "I have seen the spirits do this many times. What I wanted to see was the expression on your face as you saw it for the first time."

"You knew that this was going to happen last night, didn't you?" Harold asked.

"Yes, I did," admitted Charlotte. "I started to watch the videos just like I promised you, but then Mildred came and reminded me that I already knew that there would be nothing on the videos. She reminded me that that event had been scheduled for last night while you were sleeping."

"That was pretty sneaky of you," Harold could not contain his own laugh.

"If I told you everything in advance, you would never have had that look of amazement on your face. That look is priceless and one that I shall never forget, just as I will never forget our dances and all the time we spent together." Charlotte looked away from Harold to hide the pain and hurt that she knew was on her face as she dreaded that she and Harold had only a little over a week to spend together.

When the light show finally ended, Harold got up and quickly made a copy. They sat on the couch and talked for hours, never leaving the room. Finally Harold, with his stomach growling, said, "I think it is time for us to find some dinner. Shall we try Local Flavor tonight?"

"An excellent choice," commented Charlotte, "especially as the Balcony Bar and Restaurant is about to close. Are you ready to brave it outside on this cold wintry evening?"

"As long as you are by my side, that is all that counts," Harold smiled as he went to get his coat. When he returned to the sitting room he saw that Charlotte was already dressed to go. It never entered his mind that Charlotte, being of spiritual being, didn't need a coat. He was so much in love with Charlotte that he no longer saw her as a spirit. After all, he could feel her touch; he could feel himself touching her and he could feel the warm caress of her lips. Even during the night, he could feel her body cradled next to his just as he could feel the heat radiating from her body whenever they were dancing.

When they returned, Charlotte started encouraging Harold to take a nap. They crawled into bed and snuggled up together. Harold was in heaven and it didn't take him long to fall asleep to Charlotte's loving caresses.

As the midnight hour approached, Charlotte woke Harold with soft tender kisses.

"Oh, my, that was the most restful nap I have ever had. What time is it?" Harold asked.

"It is almost midnight, my darling"

"What did you do to help me fall asleep? I have not taken a nap since I was a kid."

"I didn't do anything," answered Charlotte. "I just snuggled next to you and into your arms. Have you not noticed that since we have been together, you have had exceptional nights' sleeps every night?"

"Now that you mention it, you're right. I have slept better every night that you have been laying beside me. You make me feel so calm and at peace." Harold struggled within himself to hide his emotions at the agony he was feeling for when he had to leave and return to The Institute of Paranormal Studies in Salem, Massachusetts. The thought of leaving his love was torture, and he believed that Charlotte felt the same way.

A knock sounded at the door. Surprised that anyone would be knocking on his door at this time of night, Harold opened the door and to his astonishment he found Simon and Mildred standing there.

"Come on you two," encouraged Simon, "Harold must be in the ballroom before they lockout the elevator and the fifth floor stairwell."

Harold, standing dressed in a suit, answered. "Yes, I'm ready. And Charlotte is always ready, in the blink of an eye, as you well know." Charlotte took Harold's arm as they walked to the elevator, up the elevator and into the ballroom. The lights in the ballroom were off and the four of them stood there in the dark so that no one would think to look inside and see Harold.

Minutes before the dance was about to begin, they heard the bartender lock the door to the fifth floor stairwell and then return to the sixth floor, where she locked out the elevator to prevent anyone from accessing the sixth floor. Then she rode the elevator down.

As Harold was about to look for the light switch for the ballroom, the room suddenly radiated in a soft subdued light. He thought that the lighting was exceptionally romantic. He then heard a voice saying, "We helped the bartender cleanup so that she would be gone quickly. You should have seen her perplexed look when the room was clean and she didn't have to do the work herself."

At exactly one o'clock, the band appeared and started playing. Harold took Charlotte in his arms and they flowed through the room. He didn't even know when the musicians ended one waltz and began another. To Harold the ballroom was empty and there was only Charlotte. It was six o'clock in the morning when the music stopped, but the two didn't hear it; they just kept dancing until Simon and Mildred shouted out that the event was over. Harold finally looked around and sure enough all of the spirits had disappeared.

Holding hands, Harold and Charlotte returned to their room. While Harold was getting ready for bed, Charlotte warmed up the breakfast they had brought home yesterday. Harold quickly gulped down the food and then they got into bed cuddling together and within seconds Harold was fast asleep, a smile never leaving his face.

Sunday afternoon arrived.

"Harold, my love, did you know it is already after one o'clock? You need to be about your work," announced Charlotte. They had been so wrapped up in each other that time had no meaning.

"Oh," moaned Harold. "Already? Where did the weekend go?"

Charlotte laughed, "Remember we danced Friday night away and slept most of Saturday. Just like you, I treasure every moment we have together."

"I love you, Charlotte, with all my heart and soul." *There, I said it,* Harold thought to himself.

"I love you too, Harold," Charlotte said as tears of joy streamed down her cheeks. "And as much as I want you here with me, I would be remiss in my duties if I didn't send you off to work. I know you will return to me soon."

Harold's emotions were riding higher than he ever thought they could as he made his way to the sixth floor. As he entered the ballroom, he immediately called out for Simon and Mildred. In an instant they appeared before him.

"Good afternoon, Harold," called Simon.

"Is there somewhere where we can talk in private?" whispered an exuberant Harold.

"Go to the park and up the stairs. We will meet you at the old Civil War cave," Mildred said excitedly, as she wondered why Harold wanted to talk to them in private.

Simon and Mildred disappeared as Harold rushed to the park. The couple was waiting, as an out of breath Harold arrived. When he got his wind back enough to talk he blurted out, "I'm going to ask Charlotte to marry me."

"Congratulations," smiled Simon.

"Are you forgetting that you are in the physical world and Charlotte is in the spiritual world," Mildred reminded him.

"No. Are you saying that it is not possible for us to get married?"

"No, I'm not saying that," answered Mildred, "but how are you going to go about it?"

"Well," Harold replied, "I thought if there was someone in the spiritual world that could marry us, that would be all we need. I don't really care if the physical world knows; I only care that Charlotte and I will know that we have been bound in holy matrimony."

"Father Daniel could perform the service," piped in Simon.

"Great. Now all I have to do is to get a ring. I know there is a jewelry store up the street called McGee's. I hope they will be open sometime before Friday."

Simon smiled as he said, "Don't worry about a ring. I will take care of that for you."

"But I really want to pick out Charlotte's ring myself," protest Harold.

"Harold, it will be the most spectacular ring you have ever seen. Trust me."

"When do you plan on proposing to Charlotte?" questioned Mildred.

"Well—I have to leave on Sunday afternoon, so I was thinking of asking her on Friday with the wedding on Saturday."

"That does not give a woman much time to prepare for the most important day of her life," interjected Mildred.

Simon burst out laughing, "Mildred, in our world Charlotte can be ready in seconds."

Mildred swatted him playfully on his arm. "Oh, you're right. I guess I was thinking of all the planning that went into our wedding."

"Then it's settled. The wedding will take place in the ballroom at one o'clock in the morning, right after the Lucky Seven Bar and Billiard Room is closed and the bartender has left," declared Simon. "Mildred and I will take care of everything. And now, Harold, you must get back to your investigation."

"Simon, will you be my best man and Mildred will you be Charlotte's maid of honor?" Harold asked.

"Of course," Simon and Mildred said in unison.

"Oh, thank you so very much. Besides Charlotte, you two have made this a most enjoyable and memorable time," Harold replied as he rushed back to the hotel.

"I STILL REMEMBER WHEN you proposed, and our wedding day," beamed Mildred.

"So do I. It seems like just yesterday. You were the most beautiful bride in the world." Simon's mind relived that day so long ago.

Mildred laughed, "All men see their brides as the most beautiful in the world. We will have to get Father Daniel to meet us here in the park so that the others will not know what is going to happen on Saturday morning; it will be a big surprise for them too, but what are we going to do about getting wedding rings?"

"Don't you worry about that, Mildred. John and I have already got plans for getting the rings," announced Simon

"You and John already made plans to get rings for Charlotte and Harold? But we just found out, just now, that Harold is going to ask Charlotte to marry him. How did you know?" questioned Mildred.

Simon shrugged, smiling. "We suspected that this might happen at the very first dance," he chuckled. "So we decided to plan ahead just in case."

"You two do know how to keep secrets."

"We didn't know if everything was going to work out the way we suspected they would, so it wasn't really a secret. There would have been no point in getting everyone's hopes up and then having them disappointed. And you know that Charlotte would have heard about it and been really excited. Then if it didn't happen, Charlotte would have absolutely been crushed," Simon explained.

"You're right. It is best if she does not know until Harold is ready. I hope that I can contain my joy. I'm so excited for Charlotte," Mildred was almost jumping for joy.

"Now Mildred, control yourself. Remember what you always say, 'Patience,'" Simon replied in an attempt to calm Mildred down.

"I know," she said, shooting him a mock glare. "Patience can sometimes be very annoying."

"Now you know how Harold has felt these last three weeks. He would have liked having all his interviews done the first week he was here, so that he and Charlotte would have had three weeks of uninterrupted bliss together." Simon tried to calm his wife's excitement, "And don't go and spoil Harold's surprise. Let Charlotte and everyone else find out when Harold is ready."

"I won't say anything," promised Mildred.

"Let's go find Father Daniel and make the arrangements with him for Saturday."

"Oh and let us not forget to get a ring for Charlotte. Harold cannot get one that Charlotte can wear from a jewelry store. And we need to get one for Harold too."

"And an engagement ring as well," Simon said with a grin.

HAROLD HAD GONE BACK to searching the hotel for his next ghostly interview. When he finally finished on the first floor, and just as he was about to return to Charlotte, Simon whispered in his ear, "park." Harold hurried down the stairs and rushed to the cave to find Mildred, Simon and John waiting for him.

Mildred excitedly blurted, "Father Daniel will marry you. We are scheduling the wedding for one o'clock Saturday morning. Everyone will be told simply that we are having another ballroom dance."

John smiled as he listened to an excited Mildred. You would have thought that it was Mildred who was getting married. John held out his hand to Harold saying, "Congratulations, son. Here is your engagement ring for Charlotte. Simon will give you her wedding ring during the ceremony and Mildred will be giving Charlotte the ring for you."

Harold frowned, "What makes these rings so special? I would have preferred picking out Charlotte's ring myself." Harold was so consumed with thoughts of Charlotte's ring that he didn't realize that he was standing in front of John Chisum.

Simon answered, saying, "These are special. You need rings that would be usable in both the physical and the spiritual world. John knew just where to find those particular kinds of rings."

Harold beamed, "John, how can I ever thank you?"

"Seeing Charlotte happy is all the thanks I need or want," answered John smiling and clapping Harold on the shoulder. You would have thought that John was the father of the bride and happy that his daughter had found a good husband.

Harold looked at the engagement ring and his eyes grew wide. His jaw dropped and he uttered, "This is the most beautiful ring I have ever seen in my life. It sparkles like the sun."

"It is very special," said John. "You will not find anything like it in the physical world."

Harold hurried back to the hotel, never glancing at either the front desk clerk or the bellman. He put the ring in his pocket as he rushed up the stairs. His exuberance carried him into Charlotte's arms and an extra long, loving kiss.

Harold made one more uneventful tour of the hotel Sunday night. His disappointment was replaced with pure ecstasy when he returned to find Charlotte anxiously awaiting his return.

Monday morning dawned with a new threat of snow in the air as Harold and Charlotte walked to Nibble's for breakfast. Several of the spiritual residents of the Basin Park Hotel smiled as they watched the loving couple. Even Charlotte didn't realize that they were being watched.

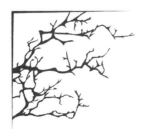

CHAPTER 10

Charlotte had her work cut out for her as she had to shoo Harold out the door and to work. As the door closed, Charlotte turned to see Mildred in the sitting room.

Mildred could not contain herself as she blurted out to Charlotte, "Before he leaves, Harold has a surprise for you."

"What is it, Mildred?" Excitement danced in Charlotte's eyes.

"If I told you, it would not be Harold's surprise."

Charlotte shot her a dirty look. "Okay, fine. I shall try to wait patiently, but I'm going to be anxious the whole time."

"It will be worth it," exclaimed Mildred, biting her tongue to prevent herself from shouting out Harold's plans.

HAROLD RETURNED FROM his trip through the hotel. He had a disappointed look on his face as he returned to Charlotte. He perked up when he saw the huge smile that his beloved was wearing.

"I take it that you didn't meet anyone to interview?" asked Charlotte.

"No, and I only have a few days left," Harold answered as his mood began a downturn as he thought about having to leave on Sunday afternoon. He hoped and prayed that Charlotte would be leaving with him.

Charlotte could barely control herself as she expected Harold to reveal his surprise at any moment, *Patience* she thought. *We all have to remember to be patient, even me.* Mildred's admonishment kept repeating in her head, just as it had to Harold. Charlotte was busting at the seams as she tried to control her own impatience.

"Don't worry. Before Friday you will have interviewed all those that you were meant to interview."

"Impatience is certainly a trait of the physical world," admitted Harold.

"Oh, trust me," she said, rolling her eyes. "Impatience is also quite prevalent in the spiritual world, as well". Charlotte laughed, thinking of her own present condition. "Let's enjoy this moment before you start your next search."

Harold smiled as he pulled Charlotte close to him.

HAROLD WANDERED AROUND the sixth floor for fifteen minutes waiting for someone to appear. And as he started down the stairs he heard a voice calling, "Harold Sangarius."

Harold turned around answering. "Yes? Oh!" Exclaimed Harold excitedly. "Are you John Chisum? I remember meeting you briefly in the park, right?"

"Why yes I am," answered the cowboy. "And yes, you did."

John was standing before Harold in the foyer. He was wearing the customary blue jeans and, of course, black cowboy boots. His shirt was a checkered blue, and a white Stetson hat covered his gray hair. A thick flowing mustache covered his upper lip and a small tuft of hair appeared just below his lower lip.

Harold said, "I was hoping to meet you at the dance, but I actually never saw you there."

John Chisum laughed, "Of course you didn't see me. You had eyes only for Charlotte, but the dance was not our appointed time to meet."

"So, you really are the famous John Chisum?" Harold asked.

"Yes, but famous for the wrong reasons. Oh yes, I knew Billy the Kid. He was a dear friend of my niece, Sally. And yes I did finance Alexander McSween and John Tunstall to open up a general store in competition with Lawrence Murphy and James Dolan. Murphy and Dolan had the only general store in Lincoln County and they were overcharging on everything and making life difficult for all the people, and thus there was a bitter feud between us and Murphy and Dolan. The feud didn't last all that long, but it certainly was the cause of what became known as the Lincoln County Wars. McSween and Tunstall were both killed before the war was over. I did give sanctuary and financial assistance to those fighting on the side of McSween and Tunstall but, all in all, that was the only part I played in the Lincoln County Wars."

"At least you did finance the war. So you did help bring victory to the people of the county," observed Harold. "And you are famous for blazing the Chisum Trail."

"Even you, an experience investigator, cannot see it. My last name is spelt C H I S U M. The name of the Chisholm Trail is spelt C H I S H O L M. Do you see it now? The Chisholm Trail was blazed by a half breed Indian by the name of Jesse Chisholm. We have no relationship. I never met Jesse. So you see, it is one thing to be recognized for what I did during the Lincoln County Wars, but still another for being given credit for something I didn't do. I'm thankful that you are here and I know that you will finally set the record straight." John sighed as he felt a great burden finally lifted from his shoulders. "When I was alive, I was more than willing to let people believe that I was the one who blazed the Chisholm Trail, but ever since my death, I have been feeling guilty about letting people believe the lie."

"Not considering the Chisholm Trail," Harold said, "you were a legend in your own time. After all, you were the king of the Pecos and you died a rich man. Your ranch stretched for 150 miles along the Pecos River. It was probably the largest ranch in New Mexico territory."

"Yes, that is all true. And when I died I left my estate to my brothers Pitzer and James. My estate at the time was valued at half a million dollars, which was quite a fortune back then. You could say that I was a self-made man. I was born in 1824 in Hardeman County, Tennessee, to a poor family. When my parents had finally grown tired of the hard struggles, they moved to Texas in 1837. I was the County Clerk in Lamar County, Texas for a little while, and didn't start learning to cowboy until I was thirty years old. I regret to say that at one point in my life I did buy a slave, a mulatto girl named Jensie. She was the only woman I ever loved. We had two daughters. When the Civil War broke out, I freed all my slaves, including Jensie. Jensie didn't come to New Mexico with me but I did provide her and my daughters a home in Bonham, Texas, and I supported them financially all my life. In the early 1860s I had accumulated over a hundred thousand head of cattle which I then drove into New Mexico territory to start my ranch on the Pecos River."

"And that's what led to your involvement in the Lincoln County wars?" Harold asked.

"The problems in Lincoln County began in the early 1870s. The war was finally triggered when Lincoln County Sheriff William J. Brady shot and killed John Tunstall. Billy the Kid, who was also known as William H Bonney, but was actually born with the name Henry McCarty, had been hired by Tunstall to help guard his herd of horses and cattle from rustlers that were employed by Lawrence Murphy and James Dolan. When Tunstall was murdered, Billy and several others set out on a course of revenge. Lawrence Murphy died of cancer in 1878 before the war ended. He was the prime instigator of the war. Even though Murphy was one of the largest ranch owners in the county and had the only general store, not to mention the only bank in the area, he continued to demand more and more power and wealth.

"James Dolan and Murphy were partners and both bore some of the responsibility for instigating the Lincoln County wars. Their rustling was not confined to Tunstall's herd. They also started rustling my herds after I helped to finance Tunstall and McSween in their mercantile and banking businesses. The Lincoln County wars finally ended in 1881."

"John, I know that you died here in Eureka Springs. Can you tell me how that came about?"

"In 1883, I discovered a tumor on my neck. In 1884 I traveled to Kansas City for treatment. The doctors cut out the tumor and I returned to my ranch in New Mexico. Soon after, the tumor had not only come back but had grown larger. That is when I decided to travel to Eureka Springs, Arkansas for their healing waters. The tumor had progressed so far that the healing waters didn't have time to work their wonders. I died on December 22, 1884. My brothers picked up my body and I was buried in Paris, Texas."

"In Texas? Then, why are you still here?" Harold asked.

"To be honest, I liked what I saw of Eureka Springs and I decided to stay here in the Perry House. The Perry House was my home until it burned down in 1890. I moved to the Southern Hotel but when the Basin Park Hotel was opened in 1905, built on the same footprint as the Perry House, I decided to leave the Southern Hotel and move into the Basin Park, and here I have been since 1905."

"That is a fascinating story," Harold said. "You certainly had a very adventurous life."

"Yes it was adventurous. If it had not been for the cancer, I could have had many more years. I was only 60 years old when the cancer ended my physical life."

"What happened to your cattle empire?" Harold asked. "It does not seem to be around any more."

"No. Rustling was still a major part of the west at that time. By 1891, my cattle empire collapsed. A man works all his life to build something, just to have it all dissolve when he is gone. It is sad, in a way, but I would do it all over again even knowing the end result."

"Some of the guests of the Basin Park Hotel have reported catching you on photographs that they took, and others have reported seeing you walk down the halls. And there were even three guests, who didn't know each other, who reported seeing you at exactly the same time as you walked from Room 310 through Room 309 and then through Room 307. What can you tell me about these reports?" Harold asked

John laughed, "They're all true. Most of us spiritual entities have been seen at one time or another. All these reports only confirm that the Basin Park Hotel truly is a haunted hotel. Fortunately for the guests, all of us "ghosts" are just mischievous. None of us are trying to do anyone harm. We all enjoy the little pranks that we do." He turned his head, as if listening to something Harold couldn't hear. "And now, you must be about your work," said John as he vanished before Harold's eyes.

Excited, Harold rushed back to his room to transcribe his interview with John Chisum.

When Harold burst into his room, Charlotte could see the excitement in his eyes. She knew he had just interviewed John Chisum. She silently sat on the couch waiting for Harold to transcribe his recordings of the interview. No sooner was Harold finished when they came into each other's arms and spent the rest of the evening together.

Tuesday came and went without any new appearances. Harold didn't mind too much because the searches didn't take too long and that allowed him to spend more time with Charlotte.

They got up Wednesday morning and prepared to get ready so that Harold could get some breakfast, when Charlotte announced that there was a new layer of snow on the ground. "The snow will not be around for very long. It will all have melted away before the day is over. Thankfully, it was not freezing rain instead."

Away they went, walking and talking, linked arm in arm, through the lobby and up the street to Nibbles restaurant. The front desk clerk, the bellman and the people on the street no longer stared at Harold as he walked linking his arm with nothing and animatedly talking to that nothing. They all knew, without a doubt, that he had lost his mind and was living in his own private dream world.

That day, Harold made three slow diligent searches of the hotel looking for his next spiritual guest to interview. Charlotte had convinced him not to give up hope and to be patient. He took his time, fully expecting that he had at least one more interview to do.

When he finally returned to his room that evening he was greeted by a happy and smiling Charlotte announcing, "We are having another ballroom dance Saturday morning at one AM, right after the bar closes and the sixth floor is deserted. I do so love dancing with you. It will be like a going away present and we will have plenty of time to say our goodbyes before you leave." Charlotte was still expecting Harold's surprise that Mildred had told her about. She was getting a little apprehensive as to whether Harold would bring forth the surprise, since Mildred had announced it a few days earlier. She had been patiently waiting and her anxiety had been building until she finally forced it out of her mind, deciding that the only important thing was the present time she was spending with Harold. A surprise would have been nice, but Harold had been her biggest and greatest surprise, especially when he said the words, "I love you."

Thursday morning after breakfast, Charlotte, as she always did, sent Harold off to work with a passionate hug and kiss. He again slowly worked his way through the hotel, room by room, floor by floor. By noon he reluctantly gave up his search. He took Charlotte by the arm and they walked to Local Flavor for lunch. Upon returning, Harold picked up his recorder and continued his hunt. As always, he took the elevator to the sixth floor to start a search from the top downward. He carefully looked over the foyer several times before walking to the ballroom. He sat on the raised bandstand platform and waited. He finally got up and went to the Lucky Seven Bar and Billiard Room. He slowly meandered to the fire escape doors at the back of the room; his eyes constantly searching every corner. Gradually he turned and slowly perused the room while he was just standing near the fire escape doors. His eyes moved across the room, back-and-forth. He stepped forward, eyes still moving, as he worked his way toward the foyer. When he reached the billiard tables, he caught sight of something in the corner of his eye. He took another look in the corner and there, sitting on the couch, was a new lovely apparition that he had not seen before.

"Hello Harold," sang the female voice. "The time has come for us to finally meet."

"Hello," Harold replied. "And what is your name?"

"My name is Silvia." Silvia sat on the couch with her leg stretched out wearing a bright red dress that stretched to her knees. Her long auburn hair was curled around her head and flowed down her back. She was a pretty lady, thought Harold, but not anywhere near as beautiful as Charlotte.

"Silvia. Yes. I think I caught a glimpse of you standing behind Abigail. You were there smiling for just a second while Abigail was accusing you of depriving her of her interview," observed Harold.

"Yes. That was me. Even though Abigail has been in the spirit world for over a hundred years, she still has many of the mental attributes of a six year old girl," laughed Silvia.

"What about your last name? You do have a last name, don't you?" Harold asked.

"Of course I do. Everybody has a last name."

"You do know that I'm recording our interview. I hope that is okay with you."

"All of us know that you are recording all your interviews. How else can you accurately relate our stories in your upcoming book if you didn't record what we were telling you?"

"Now, do you mind telling me your last name?" Harold asked.

Silvia laughed, "I don't mind. I actually have two names. I was born Silvia Marie Johnson. Most of my life I was known as Silvia Sue Starlight."

"Silvia Sue Starlight sounds like a stage name," commented Harold.

"Very astute of you," responded Silvia. "Around here my spirit friends like to also call me the trickster."

Harold's eyes opened in recognition. Simon and Mildred had mentioned the trickster. "The trickster. Sounds like you like playing tricks on people."

Silvia beamed in laughter, "Oh yes. I think it is so funny to see people's expressions when they see my handiwork."

"So what kind of things do you do that amuse you so much?"

"Lots of things. I like to unplug people's cell phones and move them to another part of the room. I also move toiletry articles from the bathroom and set them in the bedroom. The expression on people's faces is priceless. I have even levitated a book out of someone's bag and watched their expression as they saw their book floating in the air. I must have laughed for hours after that one."

"I'm sure you probably did," Harold said, grinning.

"There was one time when two ladies were checking into Room 310. They had trouble trying to unlock the door and while they were standing in the hall, I pulled one of William's tricks and tapped the one lady on the shoulder, but that was not the only thing I did to these two ladies. They stayed in that room for two days and for two days I kept them entertained. Each and every time they went in the bathroom I had moved a bath towel off the rack and onto the floor, and I even moved the toilet paper from its holder and put it on the floor too. They were such good sports. Each time all they did was hang the towel back up again and place the roll of toilet paper back on its holder. They were actually excited to have this ghostly experience." Sylvia laughed as she told the story.

"And there was another time when one lady checked into that room, Room 310. I had a good laugh over that one, too. After she put her bags down, I gently brushed her arm and she brushed at the spot thinking that there was a fly in the room. I did it a second time and laughed while she checked the room to find no flies in the room. That is when I grabbed her ankle. She actually got down on her hands and knees to see if there was anyone under the bed. She made me laugh so much that I could not resist playing another trick on her. When she went to bed I saw her put her cell phone under her pillow. Can you just imagine her surprised look when the next morning she found her cell phone lying at her feet?" Laughter filled the room as Silvia recalled that event.

"I remember one time, it was in the very room you are staying in, there was a nonbeliever staying here. She was lying on the bed watching TV and I slammed the bathroom door shut. It really surprised her. There was a really shocked look on her face. After slamming the door, I took some bobby pins out of her bathroom bag and sprinkled some of them on the floor. She got up from the bed and walked to the bathroom door. She opened it up and tried it in all kinds of positions to see if the door would close on its own again, which of course it never did. It was so funny. Then there was her look of bewilderment when she saw the bobby pins on the bathroom floor." Silvia could not contain her laughter.

"I see how all those things would be very funny to you," Harold said. He could not help but laugh with Silvia as she related her mischievous activities.

Silvia continued her story. "There was another time when two ladies were in Room 421. Around midnight, they heard what sounded like furniture being moved around in the room above them, Room 521. The next morning, the front desk manager checked to see who was staying in Room 521. It was two older ladies. One of the ladies from Room 421 had stayed in the same room on another occasion and the same thing happened. I got a good laugh over it all and the ladies happily got their ghostly experience."

"How did you manage to move the furniture around the room and not wake up the two older ladies?" Harold asked.

"Oh, that was easy. I had Abigail hum a soft, soothing melody to keep them asleep while I moved the bed around the room. Moving a king size bed around sure does make a lot of noise."

"But how did 'Silvia Marie Johnson' become 'Silvia Sue Starlight?'"

"Well... I was married once, for a very brief time. It was to a gambler by the name of Slick Bill Coleman. He was slick, all right. One night while I was working, he made off with all our money and left me without a penny. I had used the name Silvia Sue Starlight long before I met Slick. You see, I was born in the slums of New York City. I was born with the name Silvia Marie Johnson. When I was very young my father taught me the art of being a trickster, which included picking pockets, how to perform the shell game, how to stack a deck of cards and other magical things. My father was caught picking the pocket of a very rich and influential man. The man had a bodyguard who shot and killed my father. They could have had him arrested, but they murdered him instead. After that I watched my mother work herself to death in order to support us. I helped her a little bit by performing my tricks. I found I was really good at sleight-of-hand. I would manage to get some kids with money to play poker with me — I almost always won — but I had to let them win some of the time or else they would not have played with me again. My mother died when I was in my mid teens. I had my fill of the filth in New York City and set my mind on making a better life for myself than my parents had, and I used the tricks that my father had taught me to accomplish that. When my mother died I left New York and that is when I took up the name Silvia Sue Starlight. I moved around a lot, never wanting to stay in one place too long so that nobody would catch on to what I was doing. I moved from New York to Philadelphia, then Pittsburgh. I moved from there to Buffalo, Cleveland, Detroit, Chicago, St. Louis, Denver and then San Francisco. None of my marks ever knew that they had been fleeced. The saloons across the country were always a good place to find a victim, especially after they had been drinking for a while; many times they were too drunk to know how much money they were putting on the table for their poker bets. In all the years, nobody ever caught me stacking a deck of cards. Of course, it didn't hurt one bit that most of the time the men paid more attention to my pretty face and my cleavage then they did to their cards." She shot him a mischievous smile.

"I'm sure," Harold said.

"It was in San Francisco where I met Slick. I spent more time in San Francisco than any other place, and I was thinking of staying there permanently. Slick had swept me off my feet in a whirlwind romance, and we were married shortly after we had met. I really loved him," reminisced Silvia. "Turns out he was just playing me for a sucker when he saw that I was consistently winning at cards. I was devastated when I came home from a night of playing poker to find that he was gone and so was all my money. The only money I had left was what I had won that night, but it was enough to keep me going. It was rough for a little while, considering the life I had been accustomed to, but when I had saved a small nest egg, I moved to Los Angeles, the City of Angels. I had heard a lot of good things about Los Angeles. I enjoyed living there and continued to build my nest egg. The Mexican vaqueros were a great source of income, but they were also hot tempered as well. When one of them thought he caught me cheating, I decided to leave California as quick as possible. I started working my way east again through Phoenix and Albuquerque, Oklahoma City and Fort Smith, Arkansas. I didn't want to stay in Fort Smith once I heard about hanging Judge Isaac Parker. I left there pretty quickly, but while I was in Fort Smith I heard about Eureka Springs, Arkansas. I decided that the people going to Eureka Springs for the healing waters probably had money, since they had to travel a ways to get there. I had even heard about the famous and rich John Chisum and that he had come to Eureka Springs to be healed of his cancer. So Eureka Springs became my home for the rest of my life. I even had enough money and bought a home here. That was back in the early 1900s, just after the Basin Park Hotel opened."

"Fascinating," uttered Harold. "So did you die of natural causes?"

Silvia laughed, "No, not at all. None of the spiritual guests of the Basin Park Hotel died of old age. Someone caught her husband flirting with me. I was not interested in him, but she could not see that. She thought I was trying to steal her husband from her. She caught us laughing and having a beer together as we sat at a table in the Allred Saloon inside the New Orleans Hotel. She stormed through the door with a revolver in her hand. When she saw us she raised her arm and started firing. In the end, she wound up killing me and her husband. After I realized that I had entered the spirit world I moved into the Basin Park Hotel - I wanted nothing more to do with the New Orleans Hotel. As for the woman's husband, I don't know, I never saw him again ... And now Harold Sangarius, you have heard my story and now it is time for me to go."

In an instant Silvia disappeared.

Harold hurried back to his room to transcribe Silvia's interview. Charlotte watched over his shoulder as he worked. He breathed a sigh of relief when he completed that task and turned to Charlotte and said, "I suppose I will have time for one more round of the hotel this evening."

Charlotte smiling answered. "There is no need for you to do that. There is no one else for you to interview and we can enjoy the rest of the evening together."

"I certainly look forward to that," beamed Harold.

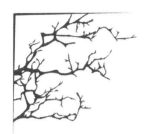

Chapter 11

Friday morning, February 3, after another intoxicating night together, Harold and Charlotte had breakfast at Nibbles restaurant, still the only breakfast place open downtown during the winter season. There was very little evidence left outside from the last snowfall. Happiness radiated from them as they returned to their room. Harold hung up his coat in the bedroom closet and as he returned to the sitting room he found Charlotte wearing an exquisite pure white gown.

For days the ring had been burning a hole in Harold's pocket. He put his hand in his pocket and excitedly fondled the ring. He pulled his hand from his pocket as he knelt before Charlotte. Looking deeply into her dazzling eyes, he presented the ring to her and asked, "Charlotte, I love you so very, very much. Will you do me the honor of becoming my wife?"

Charlotte, overjoyed with happiness, responded, "Yes, I would love to be your wife, but how can we when you are of the physical world and I'm of the spirit world?" Charlotte allowed Harold to place the engagement ring on her finger. She looked down and saw a ring that sparkled like no other could from the low light that was coming in through the window. Happiness radiated from her as her whole spirit started to glow.

"All that is important to me is to spend eternity with you. Tonight at one o'clock, Saturday morning, we will be married. Father Daniel will perform the service. Everything has already been arranged," answered an excited and exuberant Harold.

"Tonight? How can we get married so soon? I have a lot of things that need to be done to prepare," exclaimed Charlotte.

Harold could not contain his laughter, "Mildred said the same thing. Simon assured her that since you were of the spirit world that you could be ready in just a moment's notice."

"Yes, I suppose Simon is right. It is not like getting dressed and putting on makeup for the physical world." She broke into a smile. "So this is the surprise that Mildred had told me was coming. I never would have guessed, but don't you think you should have waited and proposed to me before you told Simon and Mildred?"

"Simon and Mildred are the ones who made all the wedding arrangements. And Simon and John were the ones who got me your engagement ring. I wanted to pick one out myself, but I must say that I have never seen a more beautiful ring in all my life. I could never have found a ring as special or as exquisite as this one." Harold laughed, "I'm a little surprised that Mildred was able to keep my proposal a surprise, because she was truly ecstatic when I told her that I was going to ask you to marry me."

Charlotte had to laugh herself, "I remember when she told me that you had a surprise for me. I was sure she was going to blurt it out at any moment, but as she is so famous for doing, she admonished me to be patient and to let it be your surprise. And I must say, it really was a huge surprise. You have made me the happiest woman alive... well, at least in the spiritual world."

As excited as they were, Charlotte managed to convince Harold that he needed to take a nap before tonight's big event. They lay down on the bed in each other's arms and as always Harold felt so loved and comforted that it didn't take him long to fall asleep.

Charlotte roused Harold from his slumber at 7 o'clock that evening so that they could enjoy a steak dinner at the Grand Tavern restaurant inside the Grand Central Hotel. Like the other people in town, the waitress and the bartender in the Grand Tavern stared at a man who was having an animated conversation with no one. They served him and watched him as he talked to an empty chair across from him.

As they stepped back into their room, Charlotte announced, "I'm going to leave now to get ready for our wedding. You need to get ready yourself. The next time you see me I will be walking down the aisle." She kissed him quickly, and then vanished.

Harold arrived in the ballroom just before midnight. The lights were all out and the room was empty. He slipped into the ballroom and began pacing up and down the long room. He thought to himself that one hour in the physical world could be excruciatingly slow, especially while a man was watching the clock, waiting for the most important hour of his life. Simon and John, seeing Harold pacing up and down the ballroom, made their appearance in order to make an effort to calm Harold and to help him pass those next sixty minutes.

It seemed like an eternity before they heard the bartender of the Lucky Seven Bar and Billiard Room lock up and leave the sixth floor. At that magical moment, a beautiful shining glow filled the ballroom. All the spirits were dressed in their most magnificent attire. Chairs suddenly appeared set up with an aisle down the center for the bride. Up on the stage waited Father Daniel. Simon escorted Harold to stand in front of the priest. An organ appeared on the stage and one of the musicians sat on the bench and began playing the wedding march. Harold and Simon turned and watched Charlotte, dressed in a most elegant wedding gown, being escorted down the aisle by John Chisum. She was carrying a beautiful bouquet of flowers. In front of them was Abigail Carter, sprinkling rose petals. As John escorted Charlotte onto the podium, Mildred suddenly appeared to stand beside Charlotte.

Father Daniel began:

"Welcome Family and Friends

"We are gathered here today in the sight of God and His angels, and the presence of friends and loved ones, to celebrate one of life's greatest moments, to give recognition to the worth and beauty of love, and to add our best wishes and blessings to the words which shall unite Harold and Charlotte in holy matrimony.

"Marriage is a most honorable estate, created and instituted by God, signifying unto us the mystical union, which also rests between Christ and the Church; so too may this marriage be adorned by true and abiding love.

"Who is it that brings this woman to this man?"

"I do", answered John as he placed Charlotte's hand in Harold's, and then stepped down from the stage to take a front row seat.

"Harold and Charlotte, life is given to each of us as individuals, and yet we must learn to live together. Love is given to us by our family and friends. We learn to love by being loved. Learning to love and living together is one of life's greatest challenges and is the shared goal of a married life.

"But a husband and wife should not confuse love of worldly measures for even if worldly success is found, for only love will maintain a marriage. Mankind did not create love; love is created by God. The measure of true love is a love both freely given and freely accepted, just as God's love of us is unconditional and free.

"Today truly is a glorious day the Lord hath made – as today both of you are blessed with God's greatest of all gifts – the gift of abiding love and devotion between a man and a woman. All present here today – and those here in heart – wish both of you all the joy, happiness and success that the world has to offer.

"As you travel through life together, I caution you to remember that the true measure of success, the true avenue to joy and peace, is to be found within the love you hold in your hearts. I would ask that you hold the key to your heart very tightly.

"Within the Bible, nothing is of more importance than love. We are told the crystalline and beautiful truth: 'God is Love.' We are assured that 'Love conquers all.' It is love which brings you here today, the union of two hearts and two spirits. As your lives continue to interweave as one pattern, remember that it was love that brought you here today, it is love that will make this a glorious union, and it is love which will cause this union to endure.

"Would you please face each other and join hands.

"Harold Sangarius, do you take Charlotte Ann Prichard to be your wife? Do you promise to love, honor, cherish and protect her, forsaking all others and holding only to her forevermore?"

Harold answered. "I do."

"Charlotte Ann Prichard, do you take Harold Sangarius to be your husband? Do you promise to love, honor, cherish and protect him, forsaking all others and holding only to him forevermore?"

Charlotte answered. "I do."

"Please repeat after me," said Father Daniel:

"I, Harold Sangarius take thee Charlotte Ann Prichard, to be my wife. To have and to hold, in sickness and in health, for richer or for poorer, and I promise my love to you forevermore." Harold reached over to Simon and then placed the wedding ring on Charlotte's finger.

"I, Charlotte Ann Prichard take thee Harold Sangarius to be my husband. To have and to hold, in sickness and in health, for richer or for poorer, and I promise my love to you forevermore." Mildred reached over to Charlotte and gave her a ring to place on Harold's finger.

"I charge you," Father Daniel continued:

"Harold Sangarius and Charlotte Ann Prichard, as the two of you come into this marriage uniting you as husband and wife, and as you this day affirm your faith and love for one another, I would ask that you always remember to cherish each other as special and unique individuals, that you respect the thoughts, ideas and suggestions of one another. Be able to forgive, don't hold grudges, and live each day that you may share it together – as from this day forward you shall be each other's home, comfort and refuge, your marriage strengthened by your love and respect.

"Harold Sangarius and Charlotte Ann Prichard, in so much as the two of you have agreed to live together in Matrimony, have promised your love for each other by these vows, the giving of these rings and the joining of your hands, I now declare you to be husband and wife.

"May the Lord bless you and keep you. May the Lord make his face to shine upon you, and be gracious unto you. May the Lord lift up his countenance unto you, and give you peace.

"Congratulations, Harold. You may kiss your bride." All watched the happy couple as their lips met.

Father Daniel turned to all and announced, "I present to you Mr. and Mrs. Harold Sangarius."

THE CHAIRS DISAPPEARED from the ballroom and the organ, too, as the band began to play as soon as the bride and groom had left the stage. Love songs were on their hit list for this evening. They started with "It's Magic", Martina McBride's "I love you." Their music included Ray Orbison's "Unchained Melody." On and on the band played through the night. Only Simon and Mildred were brave enough to be dance partners with Harold and Charlotte, but then only for one dance as the band played Wynonna Judd's "I'm going to love you like nobody loves you".

Simon said to Charlotte, "Harold will truly love you like nobody loves you."

"I know," smiled Charlotte with tears of joy streaming down her cheeks.

And Mildred said to Harold, "Charlotte will truly love you like nobody loves you."

"I know" smiled Harold as moisture filled his eyes.

Just before six o'clock in the morning, the band began its final song, Olivia Newton-John's "I honestly love you." When the song ended, only Harold and Charlotte were left standing in the ballroom. Walking arm in arm, feeling closer than they had ever felt in the last few weeks, they returned to their room.

The day finally arrived, February 5, for Harold to leave and return to The Institute of Paranormal Studies. After packing his bags, he and Charlotte, hugged and kissed their final tearful goodbyes. Together they rode the elevator to the lobby. As the elevator door opened, they were both very surprised to see the lobby filled with every one of the permanent spiritual residents of the hotel.

All of them had come to say a sorrowful goodbye. After Harold turned in his room key, Billy Zarta, the day time bellman, loaded his luggage into the hotel's shuttle. Charlotte linked her arm with Harold and they walked out together. At the shuttle, they embraced and kissed once more.

"Charlotte, will you please come with me? We have a wonderful home in Salem, Massachusetts. I really want you by my side forever," pleaded Harold just as he has done several times that morning.

"Harold, my dear, my love, I belong here at the 1905 Basin Park Hotel. We have all eternity together when the appointed time arrives. For me it will be just a moment in time but for you, you will have to count the years. You will always know where to find me," lovingly answered Charlotte. She knew that Harold had to continue his paranormal investigations around the country. As much as she wanted him to stay with her, she felt compelled to stay where she was.

"I will be back soon. Remember, the first weekend of every month, I will be here with you," Harold assured Charlotte.

"I will be waiting for you, my love," answered Charlotte. "I will anxiously await you. I have to remember not to be selfish; there are many other spirits across the country who will no doubt want to talk to you, too."

"I will miss you," Harold said as he sat down in the shuttle and closed the door. He could not take his eyes away from Charlotte and she could not look away from his.

The bellman/shuttle driver started the vehicle and started to drive to the Basin Park Hotel parking lot, the whole time wondering if Harold Sangarius was crazy. After all, was a person not crazy if they were talking to someone who wasn't there?

Charlotte stood in the middle of the street until the hotel shuttle was out of sight. Slowly she turned and reentered the hotel. The lobby was empty except for the front desk clerk, Simon and Mildred Garfield, John Chisum, William Arbuckle the third, Wilbur, Abigail Carter and Sylvia Sue Starlight.

There was no smile on Charlotte's beautiful face this time. Her mood didn't improve as the group expressed their sorrow - it was of no comfort to Charlotte. "Harold will be back before you know it," said Mildred.

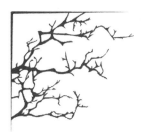

Chapter 12

Without warning, only Mildred and the trickster, Sylvia Sue Starlight, were left standing in the lobby. They looked at each other for a moment before Mildred asked, "Were you not also a fortuneteller?"

"Yes," answered Sylvia.

"You didn't mention that to Harold, did you?"

"No. I didn't think of it."

"Come on; let's you and me go to a secluded place where we will not be disturbed," said Mildred.

Knowing that the spirits freely roam the hotel, Mildred led Sylvia to the Basin Spring Park, right to the south of the hotel, and up the stairs to where there was an old cave used by injured men during the Civil War.

Mildred turned to Sylvia, "Okay, now tell me Charlotte's and Harold's future."

"I need my crystal ball to be able to see the future. Wait here and I'll be right back."

Sylvia vanished but she was only gone for a moment when she returned holding a crystal ball. She set it on the ground. Silvia and Mildred knelt down on opposite sides of the ball. They both gazed at the clear glass orb and watched it turn cloudy.

"Oh, my. This is working better than it ever did when I was alive. This is the first time I have used it since I died. Yes, there is Harold. I see him coming to the hotel the first weekend of every month just like he promised Charlotte. Oh, I see him arrive every Thursday evening and leaving every Sunday afternoon. His bosses are not too happy about it, but he is their top investigator so they are going along with it."

"If they only knew that Harold has married a ghost," laughed Mildred.

"It would be priceless to see their expressions if they ever found out," laughed Sylvia. "Oh, I see Charlotte glowing and so happy with every one of their reunions. It is like they are getting married all over again. I see Charlotte wearing her wedding dress on the days that Harold checks into the hotel. What a lovely couple they make."

"What about Christmas time?" asked Mildred.

"Let me look... Here they are. Charlotte sure looks exquisite in her Christmas dress and Harold is awed at the sight of her."

"Harold is always in awe when he sees Charlotte," laughed Mildred.

"That is true."

"What about their anniversary on February 4th?" exclaimed Mildred excitedly.

"I know their anniversary is on February 4th." Sylvia gazed into a crystal ball, "Oh! Oh!"

"What is it?" Mildred frowned.

"It is Thursday, February 1 and Harold is on the plane from Salem, Massachusetts on his way to Springfield, Missouri. The plane is going through a lot of turbulence. They are approaching the airport to land. I see heavy freezing rain and they are low on fuel, so they cannot divert to another airport. I see the landing gear being lowered. One of the engines just quit working - looks like the freezing rain is clogging the blades. The wheels just touched down on the runway. Oh, good; they are on the ground ... Wait ... No! No! ... The nose gear collapsed ... The plane just skidded off the runway and ran into one of the emergency vehicles. The emergency vehicle just burst into flames ... The fire is burning all along the plane. It looks like debris from the emergency vehicle has punctured the plane's fuel tanks. The fire is getting worse. Other emergency vehicles are arriving, but now the whole plane is engulfed in flames. The windows are melting and I see the fire spreading inside. Everyone in the plane is in panic."

"What about Harold?" Mildred was overcome with dread at the thought of Harold dying just before his first anniversary.

"There he is. Harold is in first class. The flames are worse there... Oh my God. Charlotte will be devastated," cried Sylvia.

"What about Harold? Is he going to get out of the plane?" cried Mildred.

"I'm sorry. Harold dies," came the depressed response from Sylvia.

"We must keep this a secret and tell absolutely no one. We must let Charlotte enjoy the happiness she deserves even if it is only for one year."

TRUE TO HIS WORD, HAROLD arrived at the 1905 Basin Park Hotel on the first Thursday of every month. Harold and Charlotte had eyes only for each other. Their eyes glowed as two hearts expressed the love they had for each other.

Knowing that their time together was going to be short, Mildred arranged to have a ballroom dance every Thursday night. On those days where the hotel had an event scheduled for the Ballroom on Thursdays, Mildred moved the event to the Ozark room. The dance always took place after midnight, after the bars had closed, hoping that no physical being would see Harold gliding across the dance floor with seemingly no one in his arms to dance with.

The rest of the weekend, Harold and Charlotte secluded themselves in their room, which was always Room 317. On occasion, they would walk arm in arm down the street to a restaurant and sometimes they took time to stroll through the park. People would look at Harold with raised eyebrows as they heard him talk to someone whom they could not see. They were all of the opinion that Harold had lost his mind. It was not just the fact that Harold seemed to be talking to someone, but he also had his left arm crooked as if someone was walking beside him and they were walking arm in arm. Harold never noticed their stares. He only had eyes for Charlotte.

Christmas came and Harold spent two weeks with the love of his life. Simon and Mildred were the first to comment on the happiness and the depth of love that their two friends were experiencing. All the other spirits in the hotel readily agreed. Mildred and Sylvia hid their emotional depression from the others because only the two of them knew that Charlotte's and Harold's time together was coming to an end. At least they were able to spend one Christmas and New Year's together.

Mildred and Sylvia were filled with dread as January was about to come to an end. Mildred kept wondering what they would do with Harold's body. She suspected that The Institute of Paranormal Studies would probably ship Harold's body back to Salem, Massachusetts. She shuddered at the thought, knowing that Charlotte's body was buried in the Eureka Springs Cemetery on

Highway 62. She knew that there was an empty plot beside Charlotte's grave. In her opinion, that was where Harold should be buried, but she could not figure out how to make that happen.

Mildred called Sylvia to join her in the park. "They will no doubt take Harold's body back to Salem, Massachusetts. I think Harold should be buried next to Charlotte right here in Eureka Springs."

Sylvia exclaimed, "That is a wonderful idea, but how are we going to accomplish that?"

"I don't know. I have been thinking about this for some time, but I just cannot find the answer. I'm thinking that I need to let Simon in on our secret of the future that we have been hiding."

"I think you are right," Sylvia said. "Simon may have some suggestions. I don't see any reason why we can't tell him, after all everyone will know in just a few days."

"Wait here, Sylvia. I will be right back with Simon," responded Mildred.

In just a moment Mildred had returned with Simon. They told him their secret that they had kept from everyone for the past year. Even Simon was devastated at the news and the heartache that it would cause Charlotte.

"Simon, you are the only one besides Mildred and me who know that Harold is going to die in just a few days. We have kept it a secret for a long time and I don't know about Mildred, but it is weighing heavily on my mind," said Sylvia.

"Simon, they are probably going to take Harold body back to The Institute of Paranormal Studies and bury him in Salem. Sylvia and I agree that Harold should really be buried next to Charlotte's body here in Eureka Springs." Mildred expressed her hopes and desires with a look of concern in her eyes and on her face.

Simon answered saying, "So you are saying that Harold is going to die on February 1? That does not leave us with a lot of time for making plans."

"Yes, I know. We should have told you sooner," said a depressed Mildred.

"We don't know what kind of instructions Harold might have left in the event that he should die," Simon said.

Sylvia said, "Harold was a young man. Do you really think he would have given any thought of dying? None of us ever did, and I would say that odds are that Harold didn't either. We all thought we were going to die of old age, and not be cut down in the prime of our lives."

"I suspect that Sylvia's right," Mildred said glumly.

"Then we have to find a way to convince the physical world that Harold wanted his body buried in Eureka Springs, next to Charlotte. It would be of little consolation to Charlotte, but I'm sure she would like her true love lying next to her," observed Simon.

"Do you have any idea as to how we can accomplish that?" asked Mildred.

"Well," Simon vocalized. "If we can get Harold to write a letter stating that that was his intention, then everything would work out the way you hope."

"And how do we get Harold to do that?" Sylvia asked. "It's not like we can go and tell him that he is going to burn to death on his next trip here. Can you imagine? 'Hi, Harold, you are going to die in a plane crash in Springfield, Missouri as it lands, and you are going to burn to death. You need to make arrangements as to where your body will be buried, and you must insist that you be interned in the Eureka Springs Cemetery next to Charlotte Ann Prichard.' I can see that going over real well."

"I will have to give this some thought," said Simon.

"We don't have a lot of time," emphasized Mildred

"OH, MILDRED! THERE you are. I have been looking all over for you. What do you think of this dress that I picked out to wear for our first anniversary?" asked Charlotte. "Do you think that Harold will like it?"

"That is a very beautiful dress. I'm sure that Harold will love the way it looks on you." Mildred winked at her. "I'm also sure that Harold would love it if you wore nothing at all."

Charlotte laughed too, "You're right. I have never seen a man looking at me with that kind of love and desire in his eyes as I see in Harold. I can't wait for him to get here."

"It will not be long now," smiled Mildred hiding the truth from her beloved friend.

"I couldn't be happier. I have never been so happy, ever," Charlotte said as she disappeared.

Seemingly out of nowhere came a voice, "Okay, Mildred. What is going on?"

"John, you startled me." Mildred turned toward the voice of the cowboy.

"Something is going on. I can feel it. You and Silvia seem to be hiding something from the rest of us."

Mildred took John's hand saying, "Come with me."

In an instant they were standing in front of the Civil War cave. "John, you must promise not to breathe a word of this, at least not for another few days. Something terrible is going to happen and keeping the secret has been unbearable. I finally told Simon in order to get his help."

"This obviously has something to do with Charlotte," observed John.

"Yes. In just a few days, on February 1, just three days before their first anniversary, Harold is going to die in a plane crash on his way to celebrate it with her." Tears streamed from Mildred's eyes as she told him her terrible secret.

"How do you know this?"

"From Sylvia, our little trickster. In her physical days, she would also tell fortunes using her crystal ball. I was so excited and overjoyed at Charlotte's happiness that I had Sylvia gaze into her ball and look into the future. She saw overwhelming love and happiness for Harold and Charlotte, but then she also saw Harold die in a plane crash in Springfield, Missouri while he was on his way here for their first anniversary. What has me so distraught is that The Institute of Paranormal Studies will probably have Harold's body shipped back and buried in Salem, Massachusetts. I think Harold should be buried next to Charlotte's grave right here in Eureka Springs, but we don't know how to go about making sure that that happens." She groaned with the pain of it.

"And Harold," John said, "being a young man, probably does not have a last will and testament. Yes, I see your dilemma. The answer seems to be obvious. What we need is a letter from Harold stating that he wants to be buried next to Charlotte."

"It is not like we can just go up to Harold and ask him to write his last will and testament because he is going to die in a couple of days," grieved Mildred.

"I see the problem," said John. "What we need is a letter that everybody believes was written by Harold."

"Are you saying that we should forge a letter?" asked Mildred.

"Do you think that Harold would want to be buried next to Charlotte?" queried John.

"Oh, yes. I have no doubt in my mind that that would be Harold's ultimate wish, to be laying next to the one that he loved so very much."

"Well, then, there is no other choice," declared John. "All we need to do is find someone who can forge Harold's handwriting. And don't look at me, because I'm too old to have a steady enough hand to duplicate his handwriting."

"Oh, I think Simon may be able to do that. I remember that when we were alive, he would sometimes try to imitate people's handwriting. I remember him having some fun doing that with his friends, especially when he was trying to play matchmaker. I don't think his friends or the women he sent letters to ever knew that they had come from Simon. We would both laugh at his friend's surprise and how they stumbled along in an attempt to make it seem that they knew what the letters said. Amazingly, Simon's matchmaking usually worked and as far as we know, the couples lived happily ever after."

"Then you need to talk to Simon and get him to forge a letter from Harold making the desired request. It would be best if you mail the letter but also the letter must be postmarked to a much earlier date. You might want to address it to either Curry Rich, the room's division manager, or to Jason Matthews, the general manager. Then again, it might be beneficial to mail a copy to both. You will have to go into the post office and reset the day on the stamp that they use to identify the day the post office received the letter. That way everyone will think that the letter got lost in the mail and has finally been found."

"That is a wonderful idea," assessed Mildred. "I will get Simon to work on it right away."

"I will find Simon and have him see you here in the park," said John as he disappeared.

Simon appeared a moment later. "Mildred, what is it? John said that it was urgent for me to see you in the park."

"I need your expertise, Simon. I need you to forge a letter from Harold in order to make sure that Harold body gets buried in Eureka Springs," express Mildred excitedly.

"How am I going to do that?" asked Simon. "We don't even have a sample of Harold's handwriting."

"We don't, but Charlotte does. Harold wrote love letters to Charlotte which he delivered in person on his visits. All we need to do is get our hands on those letters and then you will have a sample of Harold handwriting."

"You plan on asking Charlotte to give you the letters?" an astonished Simon asked. "I don't think she would let those letters out of her sight."

"You are right, but she doesn't mind at all letting any of us read the letters. She is so proud of her Harold and his love for her that he expresses in those letters. I have read some of those letters. I would say that they rival the letters you used to forge for your unknowing friends."

"Okay, then. Let's go find Charlotte and ask her if she is willing to let us read her letters from Harold."

Charlotte was overjoyed to share her letters with Mildred and Simon. She was so happy that her body glowed like the sun shooting out beams of love. She was so jubilant that she could not sit still. "I have to be off to share the good news with everyone, so take your time reading the letters. I will be back later to put them away."

"Hurry, Simon. You need to memorize Harold's handwriting before Charlotte returns."

With severe concentration, Simon managed to pick up a pen and a piece of paper and began copying one of Harold's letters, being patient to duplicate Harold's handwriting. Working on his third letter, Simon concluded that he could write a letter duplicating Harold's penmanship and signature. He picked up the three letters he had copied and put them in his pocket, and just in time, as Charlotte returned a moment later still walking on air in anticipation of her anniversary.

Simon and Mildred hurried off to find a secluded location where Simon could exercise his handiwork. They left the hotel walking arm in arm. They walked down to Mud Street Cafe which they knew was closed for the winter as it is every year. Here, they knew they could do what needed to be done in privacy, without being observed by other spirits.

Slowly and painstakingly, Simon worked his magic. Mildred watched approvingly over his shoulder as he worked.

"That is perfect," exclaimed Mildred with pride and excitement in her voice.

"Now, I just have to make another copy so that we can send one to Curry Rich and the other to Jason Matthews," said Simon.

"Do you think that we need to send one to The Institute of Paranormal Studies?" asked Mildred.

"That is not a bad idea," said Simon, "but we don't know to whom we would have to address it."

"Maybe it should be addressed to the CEO?"

"Yes. You are right, Mildred."

With three copies in their hands, Simon and Mildred made their way back to the hotel. Now what they needed was three envelopes in order to mail the letters and they knew just where the hotel kept its blank envelopes. With the envelopes and letters in their hand, they walked up to the post office which they knew was already closed but that was to their advantage because there would be no one to witness their handiwork. Inside the post office, Simon addressed all three letters while Mildred managed to get three stamps. She found the stamp used to cancel the postmark and after a moment managed to get the date set to two months earlier. Simon affixed the stamps to the letters and then Mildred applied the postmark stamp. With that done, they placed the letters in the out-going mail stack. Then Mildred reset the date on the postal stamp back to the present date. Breathing a sigh of relief and satisfaction that their work was done, they returned to the hotel, all smiles.

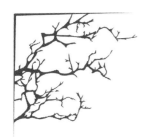

Epilogue

The next morning Simon and Mildred decided to hang out in the lobby and wait for the mail delivery. The other spirits thought that was kind of strange and some of them, including Sylvia and John, joined them in anticipation of something new happening. Only Sylvia and John knew what Simon and Mildred had been up to. Simon and Mildred could not help but display their anxiousness as they waited for the mailman. When he finally arrived, Simon and Mildred, with Sylvia and John hanging over their shoulders, stood beside the front desk clerk, Lynnette Graham, as she rifled through the mail. They were all happy to see that in the stack there was a letter addressed to Curry Rich and to Jason Matthews. Neither Lynnette Graham nor the mailman paid any attention to the postmark stamp.

They watched as Curry Rich opened his mail. He had a surprised look on his face as he read the letter. "Lyn, this is rather strange," observed Curry.

"What is it?" asked Lynnette.

"This is a letter from Harold Sangarius. It is dated two months ago. It says that if he should die, he wants us to make sure that he is buried in the Eureka Springs Cemetery next to a woman name Charlotte Ann Prichard. He even gives the date when she died, November 22, 1887."

"That is strange," commented Lynnette. "How would Harold know somebody who died in 1887? Is it possible that he met this Charlotte Ann Prichard here in the hotel?"

"Who knows?" said Curry. "He is definitely something of an odd character."

"Maybe I will do some checking to see if I can find any information on this Charlotte Ann Prichard. I think I will check the Internet for any information on her, and I might even call the Eureka Springs Historical Museum to see what they can find out," remarked Lynnette, her curiosity piqued. "If I cannot find anything, Harold is scheduled to check in on February 1, so we can ask him about it then."

"Yes. Harold has been a regular guest every month since he did his paranormal investigation, but as always, on the weekends when we're busy. It would be hard for him to do his research with so many people in the hotel. Sure makes you wonder why he comes back every month like clockwork," noted Curry.

"There is also a letter in the box addressed to Jason Matthews. It is from Harold as well," added Lynnette.

"Maybe he sent Jason the same letter to make sure that his request would be handled according to his wishes."

"But it sure is a strange request," observed Lynnette.

Charlotte had appeared and was standing with Simon, Mildred, Sylvia and John. She didn't know exactly what was going on but she heard the talk between Curry Rich and Lynnette Graham. In her exuberance she didn't hear Lynnette's last comment. What a wonderful and magnificent anniversary gift Harold was giving her. With overwhelming joy she thought of him not only lying next to her in bed but also next to her forever side-by-side, even in the grave. For him to have planned so far in advance was enchanting and electrifying. Charlotte flittered off, unable to contain her happiness.

Simon, Mildred, Sylvia and John looked at each other as they watched Charlotte filled with joy that she could not contain. Charlotte missed seeing the sorrow in their eyes.

Meanwhile, Curry Rich decided to take Harold's letter and personally give it to Jason Matthews.

IN THE EARLY AFTERNOON the next day, Thursday, February 1, the news went out over the airwaves. The flight from Salem, Massachusetts was landing at the Springfield, Missouri airport and it crashed on landing. Everyone aboard had died a horrible death as flames ravished the plane. Lynnette, who had nothing to do at the moment, had been browsing the Internet when she came across the report. She sat there, open mouthed, with an expression of utter shock. She knew that Harold Sangarius was aboard that flight. She immediately called Curry Rich and informed him of the news report. "How are you going to get the airport to release Harold's body to us?"

"I don't know. I will call Jason Matthews and let him handle it. He is the general manager, and he should be the one taking care of this, Harold's last request," responded Curry.

Simon, Mildred, Sylvia and John also heard the report. They dreaded telling Charlotte what had happened because they knew she would be devastated. Charlotte had been acting like a young schoolgirl in love but that would change when they told her. They hoped and prayed that she had not already heard the news and that none of the other spirits in the hotel would tell her.

The lobby quickly filled with all the spirits residing in the hotel but Charlotte was not among them; she was still floating in heaven. "Please, don't any of you tell Charlotte?" requested Mildred. "I will break the news to her."

"You want some company when you tell her?" asked Sylvia.

"No. I think that this is something that I need to do by myself," answered Mildred sadly. "Charlotte is not expecting Harold to arrive for another two hours, but I guess I need to go tell her now before she finds out another way."

With sad eyes and tears rolling down her cheek, Mildred looked at Simon and then went off in search of Charlotte.

Knowing that Room 317 was clean and ready for Harold to check into, Mildred appeared in the sitting room and called out, "Charlotte, are you in here?"

"I'm in the bathroom, applying the final touches. You know how I always want to look my very best for Harold."

"Can we visit for a moment?" asked Mildred. "You still have plenty of time to finish up before Harold arrives."

Charlotte danced into the sitting room all happy and aglow but when she saw Mildred's face, all that was replaced with a frown, "Mildred, what is the matter?"

"You know how happy I have been for you this last year. I think that maybe your love for Harold even surpasses the love that Simon and I have for each other." Mildred forced a smile.

"It has been the most wonderful and exciting year of my life— of my entire existence," beamed Charlotte.

"I know," frowned Mildred. "I have some news for you. Why don't you sit on the couch next to me?"

"What is wrong? I know Harold is on his way. He would not miss our anniversary for the world... Oh. No. Has something happened to Harold?" cried Charlotte in despair.

"Yes. And I wanted to tell you myself. Charlotte, Harold died in a plane crash in Springfield, Missouri, just a little while ago. He was on his way here," sobbed Mildred.

Charlotte dissolved into tears at the news. The love of her life was gone. She reached out and hugged Mildred for a long time as they each grieved Charlotte's loss. Mildred was weeping not just for Charlotte, but also for all the other spirit beings who would mourn the loss of their own relationship with Harold. None of them had ever been able to commune with a physical being the way they had with Harold, but of all, Mildred knew that Charlotte's loss would be mortifying. She didn't know how Charlotte would react when she finally understood that Harold would not be back. She had seen some spirits that had gone berserk when tragedy struck their spiritual lives. She didn't want to see that happen to Charlotte. She clung to Charlotte not wanting to let go.

Meanwhile, Jason Matthews contacted the Springfield airport and after faxing a copy of Harold's letter to them, they finally agreed to allow the body to be shipped to the Basin Park Hotel. Jason made all the arrangements to have the local funeral home pick up the body. Jason and Curry decided to have a closed casket memorial service for Harold in the ballroom. The elevator, they knew, was not big enough to hold the casket, and they would have to carry it up the stairs to the sixth floor. They also decided to place a black memorial wreath on the door of Room 317 as a special tribute, something that had never been done in the history of the 1905 Basin Park Hotel. They intended to honor him just as they were honored to have his book on display and for sale in the lobby. His book had brought much esteem and recognition to the Basin Park Hotel as truly being a haunted hotel. His book about the hotel brought guests from all over the world who wanted to perform their own paranormal investigation.

A WHOLE GROUP OF SPIRIT beings materialized in Room 317. They wanted to be there to comfort Charlotte in her loss. Simon, Sylvia and John were among them. Mildred continued to hold Charlotte tightly while she shook her head no. With utter respect for Charlotte and Mildred, they all disappeared but they didn't go far. They wanted to stay close in the event that they could be of any help.

Simon and John made their way to the front desk. They watched as Curry Rich told Lynnette to cancel Harold's reservation. Simon and John looked at each other in horror with the thought that Charlotte's grieving would be interrupted. They didn't think that it was right for Charlotte to be displaced under such circumstances. Simon, having more experience interacting with physical objects than John did, moved to the second computer. After Lynnette and canceled Harold reservation, Simon worked the keyboard and reentered Harold reservation and marked it as having been checked in.

"Hopefully they will not notice that Harold is marked as having been check in," said Simon to John.

"Maybe we just need to stay here behind the front desk to make sure that Harold's reservation stays locked in through Sunday."

"That is a great idea, John," remarked Simon. "We have nothing better to do. I'm sure Mildred will spend the weekend comforting Charlotte."

BACK IN THE SPRINGFIELD airport, the airport's emergency staff was working furiously to remove the bodies from the burned out shell of the plane. It was no easy chore, with freezing rain still pouring down and the smell of burnt human flesh. They had put chains on their vehicles but every time they carried a body to the vehicles, they themselves would be covered in ice. They moved the bodies to an empty hanger where they would later be identified and next of kin notified. At least once they had the charred remains in a body bag they didn't have to look at the blackened bodies or smell the horrendous odor of the burnt flesh.

The hours ticked by but finally all the bodies had been removed from the wreckage. The burned out hull of the aircraft was left where it was so that crash investigators from the FAA could review the damage and file their official report.

When the doors to the hanger were finally closed and lights turned off, the spirits of the dead managed to break through the body bags and emerge into the world. Everyone was talking all at once, not knowing what was going on or where they were. Their last memories were of agonizing pain as flames devoured their bodies.

"My fellow travelers," called Harold, "Be not afraid, for death is but a transition to another life. Yes, we have left behind loved ones and they will mourn for us just as we will mourn for our loss, for the life we knew in the physical world, but a new world awaits you. Go, and visit your loved ones one more time." Harold didn't add that they would have no pain or sorrow, nor would they know love and happiness anymore because he knew that it was possible. He had seen it and experienced it himself. His love for Charlotte that he had in life, he still felt even in death. He longed to feel Charlotte in his arms once more and feel the warmth of her soft lips. He thought of all the evenings that they had spent in each other's arms, dancing the night away, and he was thankful that Mildred had made such memories possible. He felt the pain of his own loss and then he thought of how Charlotte would feel when she learned that he had died and would not be there for their first anniversary.

It was in that moment that Harold realized what he needed to do. He didn't know how to do it but he stood there and willed himself to be in the Basin Park Hotel. He locked his mind on that one thought as he stood there and waited to appear in the hotel. Nothing seemed to happen. In despair, he screamed out, "Simon Garfield, help me. Simon Garfield, please help me to go to Charlotte."

SIMON AND JOHN WERE standing behind the front desk making sure that no one changed Harold's reservation. Suddenly, Simon could hear his name being called. Surprised, Simon listened more closely as the message was repeated over and over again. "Simon Garfield, help me. Simon Garfield, please help me to go to Charlotte."

Understanding dawned as Simon turned to John saying, "John, can you handle this by yourself? I must leave. Harold is calling to me. He wants me to bring him to Charlotte. He does not know how to travel yet."

"That is wonderful news. Now Harold and Charlotte can be together forever. He must be at the Springfield, Missouri airport, but I think it is best if I go get him. If the front desk people notice that Harold has been checked in, I don't believe that I can fix it, but you know how to deal with it."

"Yes. You're right, but bring him back quickly, John."

"I will be back in a flash," answered John. "And I want to be there when they are reunited."

"So do I. So do I," repeated Simon as he smiled, he was practically jumping up and down in exuberance.

"Wait. I have a thought. Do you think there is some way that you can make Room 317 disappear from their computers?" asked John excitedly.

"Maybe! I will get Charlie Hendrix down here. He's the computer geek who used to work on their computers, until he had a heart attack. He may just be able to do that," exclaimed Simon. Simon called out, "Charlie Hendrix, I need you behind the front desk."

A second pass before Charlie appeared. Simon explained what he and John wanted him to do. Charlie nodded, "I do believe that I can do that, but it might take some time for me to figure out."

"We don't have a lot of time," said Simon. "We have to be sure that Harold and Charlotte can spend their first anniversary in that room."

"I understand," answered Charlie. "I'll get to work on it right away."

Hearing that, John disappeared.

In the hanger of the Springfield airport, Harold stood there calling out continuously for Simon Garfield.

"Howdy there, partner," called John.

"John!" replied a surprised Harold. "I was expecting to see Simon. I have been calling him over and over again."

"We know. Simon heard you calling. We were standing over the front desk. When they heard that you had died, they canceled your reservation."

"Oh! No!" moaned Harold. "That room is for Charlotte and me. That is where we were going to spend our anniversary."

"Yes. We all know that. Simon managed to manipulate the computer and not only was he able to reinstate your reservation but he also has you as being checked in. Now we enlisted the aid of one of the spirits you never met, a computer guy who is trying to delete Room 317 from the computer altogether; that way you and Charlotte can spend your anniversary the way you had planned."

"I was trying to get to the Basin Park Hotel on my own, but I can't seem to move from this hangar. I have seen all of you roam all over the hotel with such ease and here I can't even get out of this room."

John answered saying, "It takes us all a little time to learn how to do that. In the meantime, take my hand, and we will be there in a jiffy."

Harold took John's hand and in the blink of an eye they were standing in the lobby of the Basin Park Hotel. He looked at John in amazement. He saw Simon standing behind the front desk. Simon moved into the lobby to greet Harold.

"Is Charlie making any progress?" asked John.

"Charlie thinks he has got it figured out. In just a moment Room 317 will disappear from their computer. He said he even added a little program so that no one will be able to add that room back into the system before Monday," laughed Simon.

"Then it is time for the three of us to pop in to see Charlotte," commented John.

Harold took the hands of both Simon and John, "Let's go. I don't want to wait a minute more."

In the twinkling of an eye, they appeared in the sitting room of Room 317. There before them, Charlotte and Mildred were still holding each other and crying a flood of tears.

Harold let go of Simon and John's hands. He stepped forward calling out, "Charlotte my love. Here I am." His arms were extended waiting to embrace her, his face wearing the biggest smile he had ever known.

Charlotte and Mildred stopped hugging each other when they heard Harold's voice. They both looked up in surprise, and then Charlotte jumped up and rushed into Harold's arms. In just an instant Charlotte's tears disappeared and love sparkled from her eyes. Her very spirit radiated a light of undying love, knowing that she and Harold would truly be spending eternity together.

(The wedding ceremony and vows can be found at http://www.vow-softheheart.com)

I HAVE BEEN AN EMPLOYEE of the Basin Park Hotel since 2008. Since then I have heard our guests tell many stories of their ghostly experiences, all of which are unexplainable. I have attempted to turn these experiences into a tale of mystery and fantasy to bring life, personality and character to the permanent residents of the hotel. Unexpectedly, this story also turned into a love story.

The 1905 Basin Park Hotel is the youngest of the five historic hotels in Eureka Springs - the others being the 1886 Crescent Hotel, the New Orleans, the Grand Central and the Palace Hotel and Bath House.

Many guests of the Basin have reported having paranormal experiences during their stay. Many of their reports are contained within the pages of this book. Their stories are written just the way our guests reported them to me.

Herein lay the tales of what might have been the physical lives of the Basin Park Hotel's permanent residents. You will laugh at the antics and cry as devastating circumstances unfold.

I hope you enjoy the stories of our permanent residents. All of them, in one form or another, await you at the

1905 Basin Park Hotel.

Made in the USA
Columbia, SC
11 August 2019